MW01114524

Mary Louisa Molesworth

Christmas-Tree Land
(Illustrated)

e-artnow 2018

Martha Finley
Christmas with Grandma Elsie (Unabridged)

F. Marion Crawford
The Little City of Hope (Christmas Classic)

Abbie Farwell Brown
The Christmas Angel (Illustrated)

William Dean Howells
Christmas Every Day and Other Stories (Illustrated)

Heoba Stretton
The Christmas Child (Illustrated)

Charles Dickens, Frances Hodgson Burnett
The Must-Read Novels for Christmas Time (Illustrated Edition)

Charles Dickens, Johanna Spyri
The Greatest Christmas Novels in One Volume (Illustrated)

E.T.A. Hoffmann
The Nutcracker and the Mouse King (Christmas Classics Series)

Frances Browne
Granny's Wonderful Chair (Christmas Classic with Original Illustrations)

Hans Christian Andersen
The Complete Fairy Tales of Hans Christian Andersen: 127 Stories in one volume

Mary Louisa Molesworth

Christmas-Tree Land
(Illustrated)

Illustrator: Walter Crane

e-artnow, 2018
Contact: info@e-artnow.org

ISBN 978-80-268-9175-8

Contents

THE WHITE CASTLE

Rollo could not help noticing the pretty picture the two made.

CHAPTER I
THE WHITE CASTLE.

'The way was long, long, long, like the

journey in a fairy tale.'

Miss Ferrier.

It was not their home. That was easy to be seen by the eager looks of curiosity and surprise on the two little faces inside the heavy travelling carriage. Yet the faces were grave, and there was a weary look in the eyes, for the journey had been long, and it was not for pleasure that it had been undertaken. The evening was drawing in, and the day had been a somewhat gloomy one, but as the light slowly faded, a soft pink radiance spread itself over the sky. They had been driving for some distance through a flat monotonous country; then, as the ground began to rise, the coachman relaxed his speed, and the children, without knowing it, fell into a half slumber.

It was when the chariot stopped to allow the horses breathing time that they started awake and looked around them. The prospect had entirely changed. They were now on higher ground, for the road had wound up and up between the hills, which all round encircled an open space —a sort of high up valley, in the centre of which gleamed something white. But this did not at first catch the children's view. It was the hills rising ever higher and higher, clothed from base to summit with fir-trees, innumerable as the stars on a clear frosty night, that struck them with surprise and admiration. The little girl caught her breath with a strange thrill of pleasure, mingled with awe.

'Rollo,' she said, catching her brother's sleeve, 'it is a land of Christmas trees!'

Rollo gazed out for a moment or two without speaking. Then he gave a sigh of sympathy.

'Yes, Maia,' he said; 'I never could have imagined it. Fancy, only fancy, if they were all lighted up!'

Maia smiled.

'I don't think even the fairies themselves could do that,' she answered.

But here their soft-voiced talking was interrupted. Two attendants, an elderly man and a young, rosy-faced woman, whose eyes, notwithstanding her healthy and hearty appearance, bore traces of tears, had got down from their seat behind the carriage.

'Master Rollo,' —'My little lady,' they said, speaking together; 'yonder is the castle. The coachman has just shown it to us. This is the first sight of it.'

'The white walls one sees gleaming through the trees,' said the girl, pointing as she spoke. 'Marc cannot see it as plainly as I.'

'My eyes are not what they were,' said the old servant apologetically.

'I see it,' —'and so do I,' exclaimed Rollo and Maia. 'Shall we soon be there?'

'Still an hour,' replied Marc; 'the road winds about, he says.'

'And already we have been so many, many hours,' said Nanni, the maid, in doleful accents.

'Let us hope for a bright fire and a welcome when we arrive,' said old Marc cheerfully. 'Provided only Master Rollo and Miss Maia are not too tired, *we* should not complain,' he added reprovingly, in a lower voice, turning to Nanni. But Maia had caught the words.

'Poor Nanni,' she said kindly. 'Don't be so sad. It will be better when we get there, and you can unpack our things and get them arranged again.'

'And then Marc will have to leave us, and who knows how they will treat us in this outlandish country!' said Nanni, beginning to sob again.

But just then the coachman looked round to signify that the horses were rested, and he was about to proceed.

'Get up, girl-quickly-get up,' said Marc, reserving his scolding, no doubt, till they were again in their places and out of hearing of their little master and mistress.

The coachman touched up his horses; they seemed to know they were nearing home, and set off at a brisk pace, the bells on their harness jingling merrily as they went.

The cheerful sound, the quicker movement, had its effect on the children's spirits.

'It *is* a strange country,' said Maia, throwing herself back among the cushions of the carriage, as if tired of gazing out. 'Still, I don't see that we need be so very unhappy here.'

'Nor I,' said Rollo. 'Nanni is foolish. She should not call it an outlandish country. That to *us* it cannot be, for it is the country of our ancestors.'

'But *so* long ago, Rollo,' objected Maia.

'That does not matter. We are still of the same blood,' said the boy sturdily. 'We must love, even without knowing why, the place that was home to them-the hills, the trees-ah, yes, above all, those wonderful forests. They seem to go on for ever and ever, like the stars, Maia.'

'Yet I don't think them as *pretty* as forests of different kinds of trees,' said Maia thoughtfully. 'They are more *strange* than beautiful. Fancy them always, always there, in winter and summer, seeing the sun rise and set, feeling the rain fall, and the snow-flakes flutter down on their branches, and yet never moving, never changing. I wouldn't like to be a tree.'

'But they *do* change,' said Rollo. 'The branches wither and then they sprout again. It must be like getting new clothes, and very interesting to watch, I should think. Fancy how funny it would be if our clothes grew on us like that.'

Maia gave a merry little laugh.

'Yes,' she said; 'fancy waking up in the morning and looking to see if our sleeves had got a little bit longer, or if our toes were beginning to be covered! I suppose that's what the trees talk about.'

'Oh, they must have lots of things to talk about,' said Rollo. 'Think of how well they must see the pictures in the clouds, being so high up. And the stars at night. And then all the creatures that live in their branches, and down among their roots, —the birds, and the squirrels, and the field-mice, and the ——'

'Yes,' interrupted Maia; 'you have rather nice thoughts sometimes, Rollo. After all, I dare say it is not so very stupid to be a tree. I should like the squirrels best of all. I do love squirrels! Can you see the castle any better now, Rollo? It must be at your side.'

'I don't see it at all just now,' said Rollo, after peering out for some moments. 'I'm not sure but what it's got round to *your* side by now, Maia.'

'No, it hasn't,' said Maia. 'It couldn't have done. It's somewhere over there, below that rounded hill-top —we'll see it again in a minute, I dare say. Ah, see, Rollo, there's the moon coming out! I do hope we shall often see the moon here. It would be so pretty-the trees would look nearly black. But what are you staring at so, Rollo?'

Rollo drew in his head again.

'There must be somebody living over there,' he said. 'I see smoke rising-you can *hardly* see it now, the light is growing so dim, but I'm sure I did see it. There must be a little cottage there somewhere among the trees.'

'Oh, how nice!' exclaimed Maia. 'We must find it out. I wonder what sort of people live in it-gnomes or wood-spirits, perhaps? There couldn't be any real *people* in such a lonely place.'

'Gnomes and wood-spirits don't need cottages, and they don't make fires,' replied Rollo.

'How do *you* know?' and Rollo's answer was not quite ready. 'I dare say gnomes like to come up above sometimes, for a change; and I dare say the wood-spirits are cold sometimes, and like to warm themselves. Any way I shall try to find that cottage and see who does live in it. I hope she will let us go on walks as often as we wish, Rollo.'

'She-who?' said the boy dreamily. 'Oh, our lady cousin! Yes, I hope so;' but he sighed as he spoke, and this time the sigh was sad.

Maia nestled closer to her brother.

'I think I was forgetting a little, Rollo,' she said. 'I can't think how I could forget, even for a moment, all our troubles. But father wanted us to try to be happy.'

'Yes, I know he did,' said Rollo. 'I am very glad if you can feel happier sometimes, Maia. But for me it is different; I am so much older.'

'Only two years,' interrupted Maia.

'Well, well, I *feel* more than that older. And then I have to take care of *you* till father comes home; that makes me feel older too.'

'I wish we could take care of each other,' said Maia; 'I wish we were going to live in a little cottage by ourselves instead of in Lady Venelda's castle. We might have Nanni just to light the fires and cook the dinner, except the creams and pastry and cakes —*those* I would make myself. And she might also clean the rooms and wash the dishes —I cannot bear washing dishes-and all the rest we would do ourselves, Rollo.'

'There would not be much else to do,' said Rollo, smiling.

'Oh yes, there would. We should need a cow, you know, and cocks and hens; those we should take care of ourselves, though Nanni might churn. You have no idea how tiring it is to churn; I tried once at our country-house last year, and my arms ached so. And then there would be the garden; it must be managed so that there should always, all the year round, be strawberries and roses. Wouldn't that be charming, Rollo?'

'Yes; but it certainly couldn't be done out of fairyland,' said the boy.

'Never mind. What does it matter? When one is wishing one may wish for anything.'

'Then, for my part, I would rather wish to be at our own home again, and that our father had not had to go away,' said Rollo.

'Ah, yes!' said Maia; and then she grew silent, and the grave expression overspread both children's faces again.

They had meant to look out to see if the white-walled castle was once more within sight, but it was now almost too dark to see anything, and they remained quietly in their corners. Suddenly they felt the wheels roll on to a paved way; the carriage went more slowly, and in a moment or two they stopped.

'Can we have arrived?' said Maia. But Rollo, looking out, saw that they had only stopped at a postern. An old man, bent and feeble, came out of an ivy-covered lodge, round and high like a light-house, looking as if it had once been a turret attached to the main building, and pressed forward as well as he could to open the gate, which swung back rustily on its hinges. The coachman exchanged a few words in the language of the country, which the children understood but slightly, and then the chariot rolled on again, slowly still, for the road ascended, and even had there been light there would have been nothing to see but two high walls, thickly covered with creeping plants. In a moment or two they stopped again for another gate to be opened-this time more quickly-then the wheels rolled over smoother ground, and the coachman drew up before a doorway, and a gleam of white walls flashed before the children's eyes.

The door was already open. Marc and Nanni got down at the farther side, for a figure stood just inside the entrance, which they at once recognised as that of the lady of the house come forward to welcome her young relatives. Two old serving-men, older than Marc and in well-worn livery, let down the ladder of steps and opened the chariot door. Rollo got out, waited a moment to help his sister as she followed him, and then, leading her by the hand, bowed low before their cousin Venelda.

'Welcome,' she said at once, as she stooped to kiss Maia's forehead, extending her hand to Rollo at the same time. Her manner was formal but not unkindly. 'You must be fatigued with your journey,' she said. 'Supper is ready in the dining-hall, and then, no doubt, you will be glad to retire for the night.'

'Yes, thank you, cousin,' said both children, and then, as she turned to show them the way, they ventured to look up at their hostess, though they were still dazzled by the sudden light after the darkness outside. Lady Venelda was neither young nor old, nor could one well imagine her ever to have been, or as ever going to be, different from what she was. She was tall and thin, simply dressed, but with a dignified air as of one accustomed to command. Her hair was gray, and surmounted by a high white cap, a number of keys attached to her girdle jingled as she went; her step was firm and decided, but not graceful, and her voice was rather hard and cold, though not sharp. Her face, as Rollo and Maia saw it better when she turned to see if they were following her, was of a piece with her figure, pale and thin, with nothing very remarkable save a well-cut rather eagle nose and a pair of very bright but not tender blue eyes. Still she was not a person to be afraid of, on the whole, Rollo decided. She might not be very indulgent or sympathising, but there was nothing cruel or cunning in her face and general look.

'You may approach the fire, children,' she said, as if this were a special indulgence; and Rollo and Maia, who had stood as if uncertain what to do, drew near the enormous chimney, where smouldered some glowing wood, enough to send out a genial heat, though it had but a poor appearance in the gigantic grate, which looked deep and wide enough to roast an ox.

Their eyes wandered curiously round the great room or hall in which they found themselves. It, like the long corridor out of which opened most of the rooms of the house, was painted or washed over entirely in white-the only thing which broke the dead uniformity being an extraordinary number of the antlered heads of deer, fastened high up at regular intervals. The effect was strange and barbaric, but not altogether unpleasing.

'What quantities of deer there must be here!' whispered Maia to her brother. 'See, even the chairs are made of their antlers.'

She was right. What Rollo had at first taken for branches of trees rudely twisted into chair backs and feet were, in fact, the horns of several kinds of deer, and he could not help admiring them, though he thought to himself it was sad to picture the number of beautiful creatures that must have been slain to please his ancestors' whimsical taste in furniture; but he said nothing, and Lady Venelda, though she noticed the children's observing eyes, said nothing either. It was not her habit to encourage conversation with young people. She had been brought up in a formal fashion, and devoutly believed it to be the best.

At this moment a bell clanged out loudly in the courtyard. Before it had ceased ringing the door opened and two ladies, both of a certain age, both dressed exactly alike, walked solemnly into the room, followed by two old gentlemen, of whom it could not be said they were exactly alike, inasmuch as one was exceedingly tall and thin, the other exceedingly short and stout. These personages the children came afterwards to know were the two ladies-in-waiting, or *dames de compagnie*, of Lady Venelda, her chaplain, and her physician. They all approached her, and bowed, and curtseyed; then drew back, as if waiting for her to take her place at the long table before seating themselves. Lady Venelda glanced at the children.

'How comes it?' she began, but then, seeming to remember something, stopped. 'To be sure, they have but just arrived,' she said to herself. Then turning to one of the old serving-men: 'Conduct the young gentleman to his apartment,' she said, 'that he may arrange his attire before joining us at supper. And you, Delphine,' she continued to one of the ancient damsels, who started as if she were on wires, and Lady Venelda had touched the spring, 'have the goodness to perform the same office for this young lady, whose waiting-maid will be doubtless in atten-dance. For this once,' she added in conclusion, this time addressing the children, 'the repast shall be delayed for ten minutes; but for this once only. Punctuality is a virtue that cannot be exaggerated.'

Rollo and Maia looked at each other; then both followed their respective guides.

'Is my lady cousin angry with me?' Maia ventured timidly to inquire. 'We did not know-we could not help it. I suppose the coachman came as fast as he could.'

'Perfectly, perfectly, Mademoiselle,' replied Delphine in a flutter. Poor thing, she had once been French-long, long ago, in the days of her youth, which she had well-nigh forgotten. But she still retained some French expressions and the habit of agreeing with whatever was said to her, which she believed to show the highest breeding. 'Of course Mademoiselle could not help it.'

'Then why is my cousin angry?' said Maia, again looking up with her bright brown eyes.

'My lady Venelda angry?' repeated Delphine, rather embarrassed how to reconcile her loyalty to her patroness, to whom she was devotedly attached, with courtesy to Maia. 'Ah, no! My lady is never angry. Pardon my plain speaking.'

'Oh, then, I mistook, I suppose,' said Maia, considerably relieved. 'I suppose some people seem angry when they're not, till one gets to know them.'

And then Maia, who was of a philosophic turn of mind, made Nanni hurry to take off her wraps and arrange her hair, that she might go down to supper: 'for I'm dreadfully hungry,' she added, 'and it's very funny downstairs, Nanni,' she went on. 'It's like something out of a book, hundreds of years ago. I can quite understand now why father told us to be so particular always to say "our lady cousin," and things like that. Isn't it funny, Nanni?'

Nanni's spirits seemed to have improved.

'It is not like home, certainly, Miss Maia,' she replied. 'But I dare say we shall get on pretty well. They seem very kind and friendly downstairs in the kitchen, and there was a very nice supper getting ready. And then, I'm never one to make the worst of things, whatever that crabbed old Marc may say.'

Maia was already on her way to go. She only stopped a moment to glance round the room. It was large, but somewhat scantily furnished. The walls white, like the rest of the house, the floor polished like a looking-glass. Maia's curtainless little bed in one corner looked disproportionately small. The child gave a little shiver.

'It feels very cold in this big bare room,' she said. 'I hope you and Rollo aren't far off.'

'I don't know for Master Rollo,' Nanni replied. 'But this is *my* room,' and she opened a door leading into a small chamber, neatly but plainly arranged.

'Oh, that's very nice,' said Maia, approvingly. 'If Rollo's room is not far off, we shall not feel at all lonely.'

Her doubts were soon set at rest, for, as she opened the door, Rollo appeared coming out of a room just across the passage.

'Oh, that's your room,' said Maia. 'I didn't see where you went to. I was talking to Mademoiselle Delphine. I'm so glad you're so near, Rollo.'

'Yes,' said Rollo. 'These big bare rooms aren't like our rooms at home. I should have felt rather lonely if I'd been quite at the other end of the house.'

Then they took each other's hand and went slowly down the uncarpeted white stone staircase.

'Rollo,' said Maia, nodding her head significantly as if in the direction of the dining-hall, 'do you think we shall like her? Do you think she's going to be kind?'

Rollo hesitated.

'I think she'll be kind. Father said she would. But I don't think she cares about children, and we'll have to be very quiet, and all that.'

'The best thing will be going long walks in the woods,' said Maia.

'Yes, if she'll let us,' replied Rollo doubtfully.

'Well, I'll tell you how to do. We'll show her we're awfully good and sensible, and then she won't be afraid to let us go about by ourselves. Oh, Rollo, those lovely Christmas-tree woods! We can't feel dull if only we may go about in the woods!'

'Well, then, let's try, as you say, to show how very good and sensible we are,' said Rollo.

And with this wise resolution the two children went in to supper.

CHAPTER II
IN THE FIR-WOODS.

...'Gloomy shades, sequestered deep,
....whence one could only see

Stems thronging all around.'...

KEATS.

Supper was a formal and stately affair. The children were placed one on each side of their cousin, and helped to such dishes as she considered suitable, without asking them what they liked. But they were not greedy children, and even at their own home they had been accustomed to much more strictness than is *nowadays* the case, my dear children, for those were still the days when little people were expected to be 'seen but not heard,' to 'speak when they were spoken to,' but not otherwise. So Rollo and Maia were not unduly depressed, especially as there was plenty of amusement for their bright eyes in watching the queer, pompous manners of Lady Venelda's attendants, and making notes to discuss together afterwards on the strange and quaint china and silver which covered the table, and even in marvelling at the food itself, which, though all good, was much of it perfectly new to them.

Now and then their hostess addressed a few words to them about their journey, their father's health when they had left him, and such things, to which Rollo and Maia replied with great propriety. Lady Venelda seemed pleased.

'They have been well brought up, I see. My cousin has not neglected them,' she said in a low voice, as if speaking to herself, which was a habit of hers. Rollo and Maia exchanged signals with each other at this, which they had of course overheard, and each understood as well as if the other had said it aloud, that the meaning of the signals was, 'That is right. If we go on like this we shall soon get leave to ramble about by ourselves.'

After supper Lady Venelda told the children to follow her into what she chose to call her retiring-room. This was a rather pretty room at the extreme end of the long white gallery, but unlike that part of the castle which the children had already seen. The walls were not white, but hung with tapestry, which gave it a much warmer and more comfortable look. One did not even here, however, get rid of the poor deer, for the tapestry all round the room represented a hunting-scene, and it nearly made Maia cry, when she afterwards examined it by daylight, to see the poor chased creatures, with the cruel dogs upon them and the riders behind lashing their horses, and evidently shouting to the hounds to urge them on. It was a curious subject to have chosen for a lady's boudoir, but Lady Venelda's tastes were guided by but one rule-the most profound respect and veneration for her ancestors, and as they had seen fit thus to decorate the prettiest room in the castle, it would never have occurred to her to alter it.

She seated herself on an antlered couch below one of the windows, which by day commanded a beautiful view of the wonderful woods, but was now hidden by rather worn curtains of a faded blue, the only light in the room coming from a curiously-shaped oil lamp suspended from the ceiling, which illumined but here and there parts of the tapestry, and was far too dim to have made it possible to read or work. But it was not much time that the lady of the castle passed in her bower, and seldom that she found leisure to read, for she was a very busy and practical person, managing her large possessions entirely for herself, and caring but little for the amusements or occupations most ladies take pleasure in. She beckoned to the children to come near her.

'You are tired, I dare say,' she said graciously. 'At your age I remember the noble Count, my father, took me once a journey lasting two or three days, and when I arrived at my destination I slept twelve hours without awaking.'

'Oh, but we shall not need to sleep as long as that,' said Rollo and Maia together. 'We shall be quite rested by to-morrow morning;' at which the Lady Venelda smiled, evidently pleased, even though they had spoken so quickly as *almost* to interrupt her.

'That is well,' she said. 'Then I shall inform you of how I propose to arrange your time, at once, though I had intended giving orders that you should not be awakened till eight o'clock. At what hour do you rise at home?'

'At seven, lady cousin,' said Rollo.

'That is not very early,' she replied. 'However, as it is but for a time that you are confided to my care, I cannot regulate everything exactly as I could wish.'

'We would like to get up earlier,' said Maia hastily. 'Perhaps not *to-morrow*,' she added.

'I will first tell you my wishes,' said Lady Venelda loftily. 'At eight o'clock prayers are read to the household in the chapel. You will already have had some light refreshment. At nine you will have instruction from Mademoiselle Delphine for one hour. At ten the chaplain will take her place for two hours. At twelve you may walk in the grounds round the house for half an hour. At one we dine. At two you shall have another hour from Mademoiselle Delphine. From three to five you may walk with your attendants. Supper is at eight; and during the evening you may prepare your tasks for the next day.'

Rollo and Maia looked at each other. It was not so very bad; still it sounded rather severe. Rollo took courage.

'If we get up earlier and do our tasks, may we stay out later sometimes?' he inquired.

'Sometimes-if the weather is very fine and you have been very industrious,' their cousin replied.

'And,' added Maia, emboldened by this success, 'may we sometimes ramble alone all about the woods? We do so love the woods,' she continued, clasping her hands.

Now, if Lady Venelda herself had a weakness, it was for these same woods. They were to her a sort of shrine dedicated to the memory of her race, for the pine forests of that country had been celebrated as far back as there was any record of its existence. So, though she was rather startled at Maia's proposal, she answered graciously still:

'They are indeed beautiful, my child. Beautiful and wonderful. There have they stood in their solemn majesty for century after century, seeing generation after generation of our race pass away while yet they remain. They and I alone, my children. I, the last left of a long line!'

Her voice trembled, and one could almost have imagined that a tear glittered in her blue eyes. Maia, and Rollo too, felt very sorry for her.

'Dear cousin,' said the girl, timidly touching her hand, 'are we not a little *little*, relations to you? Please don't say you are all alone. It sounds so very sad. Do let Rollo and me be like your little boy and girl.'

Lady Venelda smiled again, and this time her face really grew soft and gentle.

'Poor children,' she said, in the peculiar low voice she always used when speaking to herself, and apparently forgetting the presence of others, 'poor children, they too have suffered. They have no mother!' Then turning to Maia, who was still gently stroking her hand: 'I thank you, my child, for your innocent sympathy,' she said, in her usual tone. 'I rejoice to have you here. You will cheer my solitude, and at the same time learn no harm, I feel sure, from the associations of this ancient house.'

Maia did not quite understand her, but as the tone sounded kind, she ventured to repeat, as she kissed her cousin's hand for good-night, 'And you will let us ramble about the woods if we are very good, won't you? And *sometimes* we may have a whole holiday, mayn't we?'

Lady Venelda smiled.

'All will depend on yourselves, my child,' she said.

But Rollo and Maia went upstairs to bed very well satisfied with the look of things.

They *meant* to wake very early, and tried to coax Nanni to promise to go out with them in the morning before prayers, but Nanni was cautious, and would make no rash engagements.

'*I* am very tired, Miss Maia,' she said, 'and I am sure you must be if you would let yourself think so. I hope you will have a good long sleep.'

She was right. After all, the next morning Rollo and Maia had hardly time to finish their coffee and rolls before the great bell in the courtyard clanged for prayers, and they had to hurry to the chapel not to be too late. Prayers over, they were taken in hand by Mademoiselle Delphine, and then by the old chaplain, till, by twelve o'clock, when they were sent out for a little fresh air before dinner, they felt more sleepy and tired than the night before.

'I don't care to go to the woods now,' said Maia dolefully. 'I am so tired-ever so much more tired than with lessons at home.'

'So am I,' said Rollo. 'I don't know what is the matter with me,' and he seated himself disconsolately beside his sister on a bench overlooking the stiff Dutch garden at one side of the castle.

'Come-how now, my children?' said a voice beside them; 'why are you not running about, instead of sitting there like two old invalids?'

'We are so tired,' said both together, looking up at the new-comer, who was none other than the short, stout old gentleman who had been introduced to them as Lady Venelda's physician.

'Tired; ah, well, to be sure, you have had a long journey.'

'It is not only that. We weren't so tired this morning, but we've had such a lot of lessons.' 'Mademoiselle Delphine's French is very hard,' said Maia; 'and Mr. —I forget his name-the chaplain says the Latin words quite differently from what I've learnt before,' added Rollo.

The old doctor looked at them both attentively.

'Come, come, my children, you must not lose heart. What would you say to a long afternoon in the woods and no more lessons to-day, if I were to ask the Lady Venelda to give you a holiday?'

The effect was instantaneous. Both children jumped up and clapped their hands.

'Oh, thank you, thank you, Mr. —Doctor,' they said, for they had not heard his name. 'Yes, that is just what we would like. It did not seem any good to go to the woods for just an hour or two. And, oh, Mr. Doctor, do ask our cousin to give us one holiday a week-we always have that at home. It is so nice to wake up in the morning and know there are *no* lessons to do! And we should be so good all the other days.'

'Ah, well,' said the old doctor, 'we shall see.'

But he nodded his head, and smiled, and looked so like a good-natured old owl, that Rollo and Maia felt very hopeful.

At dinner, where they took their places as usual at each side of their cousin, nothing was said till the close. Then Lady Venelda turned solemnly to the children:

'You have been attentive at your lessons, I am glad to hear,' she said; 'but you are doubtless still somewhat tired with your journey. My kind physician thinks some hours of fresh air would do you good. I therefore shall be pleased for you to spend all the afternoon in the woods-there will be no more lessons to-day.'

'Oh, thank you, thank you,' repeated the children, and Maia glanced at her cousin with some thought of throwing her arms round her and kissing her, but Lady Venelda looked so very stiff and stately that she felt her courage ebb.

'It is better only to kiss her when we are alone with her,' she said afterwards to Rollo, in which he agreed.

But they forgot everything except high spirits and delight when, half an hour later, they found themselves with Nanni on their way to the longed-for woods.

'Which way shall we go?' said Maia; and indeed it was a question for consideration. For it was not on one side only that there were woods, but on every side, far as the eye could reach, stretched out the wonderful forests. The white castle stood on raised ground, but in the centre of a circular valley, so that to reach the outside world one had first to descend and then rise again; so the entrance to the woods was sloping, for the castle hill was bare of trees, which began only at its base.

'Which way?' repeated Rollo; 'I don't see that it matters. We get into the woods every way.'

'Except over there,' said Maia, pointing to the road by which they had come, gleaming like a white ribbon among the trees, which had been thinned a little in that direction.

'Well, we don't want to go there,' said Rollo, but before he had time to say more Maia interrupted him.

'Oh, Rollo, let's go the way that we saw the little cottage. No, I don't mean that we saw the cottage, but we saw the smoke rising, and we were sure there was a cottage. It was-let me see — —' and she tried to put herself in the right direction; 'yes, it was on my left hand-it must be on that side,' and she pointed where she meant.

Rollo did not seem to care particularly about the real or imaginary cottage, but as to him all roads were the same in this case, seeing all led to the woods, he made no objection, and a few minutes saw the little party, already in the shade of the forest, slowly making their way upwards. It was milder than the day before; indeed, for early spring it was very mild. The soft afternoon sunshine came peeping through the branches, the ground was beautifully dry, and their steps made a pleasant crackling sound, as their feet broke the innumerable little twigs which, interspersed with moss and the remains of last year's leaves, made a nice carpet to walk on.

'Let us stand still a moment,' said Maia, 'and look about us. How delicious it is! *What* flowers there will be in a little while! Primroses, I am sure, and violets, and later on periwinkle and cyclamen, I dare say.'

A sigh from Nanni interrupted her.

'What is the matter?' said the children.

'I am so tired, Miss Maia,' said poor Nanni. 'I haven't got over the journey, and I was so afraid of being late this morning that I got up I don't know how early-they told me in the kitchen that their lady was so angry if any one was late. I think if I were to sit down on this nice mossy ground I should really go to sleep.'

'*Poor* Nanni!' said Maia, laughing. 'Well, do sit down, only I think you'd better not go to sleep; you might catch cold.'

'It's beautifully warm here among the trees, somehow,' said Nanni. 'Well, then, shall I just stay here and you and Master Rollo play about? You won't go far?'

'You *would* get a nice scolding if we were lost,' said Rollo mischievously.

'Don't tease her, Rollo,' said Maia; adding in a lower tone, 'If you do, she'll persist in coming with us, and it will be such fun to run about by ourselves.' Then turning to Nanni, 'Don't be afraid of us, Nanni; we shan't get lost. You may go to sleep for an hour or two if you like.'

The two children set off together in great glee. Here and there among the trees there were paths, or what looked like paths, some going upwards till quite lost to view, some downwards, — all in the most tempting zigzag fashion.

'I should like to explore all the paths one after the other, wouldn't you?' said Maia.

'I expect they all lead to nowhere in particular,' said Rollo, philosophically.

'But we want to go somewhere in particular,' said Maia; 'I want to find the cottage, you know. I am sure it must be *somewhere* about here.'

'Upwards or downwards-which do you think?' said Rollo. 'I say, Maia, suppose you go downwards and I upwards, and then we can meet again here and say if we've found the cottage or had any adventures, like the brothers in the fairy tales.'

'No,' said Maia, drawing nearer Rollo as she spoke; 'I don't want to go about alone. You know, though the woods are so nice they're *rather* lonely, and there are such queer stories about forests always. There must be queer people living in them, though we don't see them. Gnomes and brownies down below, very likely, and wood-spirits, perhaps. But I think about the gnomes is the most frightening, don't you, Rollo?'

'I don't think any of it's frightening,' he replied. But he was a kind boy, so he did not laugh at Maia, or say any more about separating. 'Which way shall we go, then?'

'Oh, we'd better go on upwards. There can't be much forest downwards, for we've come nearly straight up. We'd get out of the wood directly.'

They went on climbing therefore for some way, but the ascent became quickly slighter, and in a short time they found themselves almost on level ground.

'We can't have got to the top,' said Rollo. 'This must be a sort of ledge on the hillside. However, I begin to sympathise with Nanni-it's nice to get a rest,' and he threw himself down at full length as he spoke. Maia quickly followed his example.

'We shan't do much exploring at this rate,' she said.

'No,' Rollo agreed; 'but never mind. Isn't it nice here, Maia? Just like what father told us, isn't it? The scent of the fir-trees is so delicious too.'

It was charmingly sweet and peaceful, and the feeling of mystery caused by the dark shade of the lofty trees, standing there in countless rows as they had stood for centuries, the silence only broken by the occasional dropping of a twig or the flutter of a leaf, impressed the children in a way they could not have put in words. It was a sort of relief when a slight rustle in the branches overhead caught their attention, and looking up, their quick eyes saw the bright brown, bushy tail of a squirrel whisking out of sight.

Up jumped Maia, clapping her hands.

'A squirrel, Rollo, did you see?'

'Of course I did, but you shouldn't make such a noise. We might have seen him again if we'd been quite quiet. I wonder where his home is.'

'So do I. *How* I should like to see a squirrel's nest and all the little ones sitting in a row, each with a nut in its two front paws! *How* nice it would be to have the gift of understanding all the animals say to each other, wouldn't it?'

'Yes,' said Rollo, but he stopped suddenly. 'Maia,' he exclaimed, 'I believe I smell burning wood!' and he stood still and sniffed the air a little. 'I shouldn't wonder if we're near the cottage.'

'Oh, do come on, then,' said Maia eagerly. 'Yes-yes; I smell it too. I hope the cottage isn't on fire, Rollo. Oh, no; see, it must be a bonfire,' for, as she spoke, a smouldering heap of leaves and dry branches came in sight some little way along the path, and in another moment, a few yards farther on, a cottage actually appeared.

Such an original-looking cottage! The trees had been cleared for some distance round where it stood, and a space enclosed by a rustic fence of interlaced branches had been planted as a garden. A very pretty little garden too. There were flower-beds in front, already gay with a few early blossoms, and neat rows of vegetables and fruit-bushes at the back. The cottage was built of wood, but looked warm and dry, with deep roof and rather small high-up windows. A little path, bordered primly by a thick growing mossy-like plant, led up to the door, which was closed. No smoke came out of the chimney, not the slightest sound was to be heard. The children looked at each other.

'What a darling little house!' said Maia in a whisper. 'But, Rollo, do you think there's anybody there? Can it be *enchanted*, perhaps?'

Rollo went on a few steps and stood looking at the mysterious cottage. There was not a sound to be heard, not the slightest sign of life about the place; and yet it was all in such perfect order that it was impossible to think it deserted.

'The people must have gone out, I suppose,' said Rollo.

'I wonder if the door is locked,' said Maia. 'I am *so* thirsty, Rollo.'

'Let's see,' Rollo answered, and together the two children opened the tiny gate and made their way up to the door. Rollo took hold of the latch; it yielded to his touch.

'It's not locked,' he said, looking back at his sister, and he gently pushed the door a little way open. 'Shall I go in?' he said.

Maia came forward, walking on her tiptoes.

'Oh, Rollo,' she whispered, '*suppose* it's enchanted, and that we never get out again.'

But all the same she crept nearer and nearer to the tempting half-open door.

CHAPTER III
THE MYSTERIOUS COTTAGE.

> "'A pretty cottage 'tis indeed,"
> Said Rosalind to Fanny,
> "But yet it seems a little strange,
>
> I trust there's naught uncanny.'"

The Wood-Fairies.

Rollo pushed a little more, and still a little. No sound was heard-no voice demanded what they wanted; they gathered courage, till at last the door stood sufficiently ajar for them to see inside. It was a neat, plain, exceedingly clean, little kitchen which stood revealed to their view. Rollo and Maia, with another glance around them, another instant's hesitation, stepped in.

The floor was only sanded, the furniture was of plain unvarnished deal, yet there was something indescribably dainty and attractive about the room. There was no fire burning in the hearth, but all was ready laid for lighting it, and on the table, covered with a perfectly clean, though coarse cloth, plates and cups for a meal were set out. It seemed to be for three people. A loaf of brownish bread, and a jug filled with milk, were the only provisions to be seen. Maia stepped forward softly and looked longingly at the milk.

'Do you think it would be wrong to take some, Rollo?' she said. 'I *am* so thirsty, and they must be nice people that live here, it looks so neat.' But just then, catching sight of the three chairs drawn round the table, as well as of the three cups and three plates upon it, she drew back with a little scream. 'Rollo,' she exclaimed, her eyes sparkling, half with fear, half with excitement, 'I do believe we've got into the cottage of *the three bears.*'

'Rollo,' she exclaimed, her eyes sparkling, half with fear, half with excitement, 'I do believe
we've got into the cottage of the three bears.'

Rollo burst out laughing, though, to tell the truth, he was not quite sure if his sister was
in fun or earnest.

'Nonsense, Maia!' he said. 'Why, that was hundreds of years ago. You don't suppose the
bears have gone on living ever since, do you? Besides, it wouldn't do at all. See, there are two

smaller chairs and one arm-chair here. Two small cups and one big one. It's just the wrong way for the bears. It must be two children and one big person that live here.'

Maia seemed somewhat reassured.

'Do you think I may take a drink of milk, then?' she said. 'I am *so* thirsty.'

'I should think you might,' said Rollo. 'You see we can come back and pay for it another day when they're at home. If we had any money we might leave it here on the table, to show we're honest. But we haven't any.'

'No,' said Maia, as she poured out some milk, taking care not to spill any on the tablecloth, 'not a farthing. Oh, Rollo,' she continued, '*such* delicious milk! Won't you have some?'

'No; I'm not thirsty,' he replied. 'See, Maia, there's another little kitchen out of this—for washing dishes in —a sort of scullery,' for he had opened another door as he spoke.

'And, oh, Rollo,' said Maia, peering about, 'see, there's a little stair. Oh, *do* let's go up.'

It seemed a case of 'in for a penny, in for a pound.' Having made themselves so much at home, the children felt inclined to go a little farther. They had soon climbed the tiny staircase and were rewarded for their labour by finding two little bed-rooms, furnished just alike, and though neat and exquisitely clean, as plain and simple as the kitchen.

'Really, Rollo,' said Maia, 'this house might have been built by the fairies for us two, and see, isn't it odd? the beds are quite small, like ours. I don't know where the big person sleeps whom the arm-chair and the big cup downstairs are for.'

'Perhaps there's another room,' said Rollo, but after hunting about they found there was nothing more, and they came downstairs again to the kitchen, more puzzled than ever as to whom the queer little house could belong to.

'We'll come back again, the very first day we can,' said Maia, 'and tell the people about having taken the milk,' and then they left the cottage, carefully closing the door and gate behind them, and made their way back to where they had left Nanni. It took them longer than they had expected—either they mistook their way, or had wandered farther than they had imagined. But Nanni had suffered no anxiety on their account, for, even before they got up to her, they saw that she was enjoying a peaceful slumber.

'Poor thing!' said Maia. 'She must be very tired. I never knew her so sleepy before. Wake up, Nanni, wake up,' she went on, touching the maid gently on the shoulder. Up jumped Nanni, rubbing her eyes, but looking nevertheless very awake and good-humoured.

'Such a beautiful sleep as I've had, to be sure,' she exclaimed.

'Then you haven't been wondering what had become of us?' said Rollo.

'Bless you, no, sir,' replied Nanni. 'You haven't been very long away, surely? I never did have such a beautiful sleep. There must be something in the air of this forest that makes one sleep. And such lovely dreams! I thought I saw a lady all dressed in green—dark green and light green, —for all the world like the fir-trees in spring, and with long light hair. She stooped over me and smiled, as if she was going to say something, but just then I awoke and saw Miss Maia.'

'And what do you think *we've* seen?' said Maia. 'The dearest little cottage you can fancy. Just like what Rollo and I would like to live in all by ourselves. And there was nobody there; wasn't it queer, Nanni?'

Nanni was much impressed, but when she had heard all about the children's adventure she grew a little frightened.

'I hope no harm will come of it,' she said. 'If it were a witch's cottage;' and she shivered.

'Nonsense, Nanni,' said Rollo; 'witches don't have cottages like that, —all so bright and clean, and delicious new milk to drink.'

But Nanni was not so easily consoled. 'I hope no harm may come of it,' she repeated.

By the lengthening shadows they saw that the afternoon was advancing, and that, if they did not want to be late for dinner, they must make the best of their way home.

'It would not do to be late to-day —the first time they have let us come out by ourselves,' said Maia sagely. 'If we are back in very good time perhaps Lady Venelda will soon let us come again.'

They *were* back in very good time, and went down to the dining-hall, looking very fresh and neat, as their cousin entered it followed by her ladies.

'That is right,' said Lady Venelda graciously.

'You look all the better for your walk, my little friends,' said the old doctor. 'Come, tell us what you think of our forests, now you have seen the inside of them.'

'They are lovely,' said both children enthusiastically. 'I should like to *live* there,' Maia went on; 'and, oh, cousin, we saw the dearest little cottage, *so* neat and pretty! I wonder who lives there.'

'You went to the village, then,' Lady Venelda replied. 'I did not think you would go in that direction.'

'No,' said Rollo, 'we did not go near any village. It was a cottage quite alone, over that way,' and he pointed in the direction he meant.

Lady Venelda looked surprised and a little annoyed.

'I know of no cottage by itself. I know of no cottages, save those in my own village. You must have been mistaken.'

'Oh, no, indeed,' said Maia, 'we could not be mistaken, for we —— —'

'Young people should not contradict their elders,' said Lady Venelda freezingly, and poor Maia dared say no more. She was very thankful when the old doctor came to the rescue.

'Perhaps,' he said good-naturedly, 'perhaps our young friends sat down in the forest and had a little nap, in which they *dreamt* of this mysterious cottage. You are aware, my lady, that the aromatic odours of our delightful woods are said to have this tendency.'

Rollo and Maia looked at each other. 'That's true,' the look seemed to say, for the old doctor's words made them think of Nanni's beautiful dream. Not that *they* had been asleep, oh, no, that was impossible.

Everything about the cottage had been so real and natural. And besides, as Maia said afterwards to Rollo, 'People don't dream *together* of exactly the same things at exactly the same moment, as if they were reading a story-book,' with which Rollo of course agreed.

Still, at the time, they were not sorry that their cousin took up the doctor's idea, for she had seemed so very vexed before he suggested it.

'To be sure,' she replied graciously; 'that explains it. I have often heard of that quality of our wonderful woods. No doubt-tired as they were too-the children fell asleep without knowing it. Just so; but young people must never contradict their elders.'

The children dared not say any more, and, indeed, just then it would have been no use.

'She would not have believed anything we said about it,' said Maia as they went upstairs to their own rooms. 'But it isn't nice not to be allowed to tell anything like that. *Father* always believes us.'

'Yes,' said Rollo thoughtfully. 'I don't quite understand why Lady Venelda should have taken us up so about it. I don't much like going back to the cottage without leave-at least without telling her about it, and yet we *must* go. It would be such a shame not to pay for the milk.'

'Yes,' said Maia, 'and they might think there had been *robbers* there while they were out. Oh, we must go back!'

But their perplexities were not decreased by what Nanni had to say to them.

'Oh, Master Rollo and Miss Maia!' she exclaimed, 'we should be *very* thankful that no harm came to you this afternoon. I've been speaking to them in the kitchen about where you were, and, oh, but it must be an uncanny place! No one knows who lives there, though 'tis said about 'tis a witch. And the queer thing is, that 'tis but very few that have ever seen the cottage at all. Some have seen it and told the others about it, and when they've gone to look, no cottage could they find. Lady Venelda's own maid is one of those who was determined to find it, but she never could. And my Lady herself was so put out about it that she set off to look for it one day, —for no one has a right to live in the woods just hereabout without her leave, —and she meant to turn the people, whoever they were, about their business. But 'twas all for no use. She sought far and wide; ne'er a cottage could she find, and she wandered about the woods near a whole day for no use. Since then she is that touchy about it that, if any one dares but to mention a cottage hereabouts, save those in the village, it quite upsets her.'

Rollo and Maia looked at each other, but something made them feel it was better to say little before Nanni.

'So I do beg you never to speak about the cottage to my Lady,' Nanni wound up.

'We don't want to speak about it to her,' said Rollo drily.

'And you won't want to go there again, I do hope,' the maid persisted. 'Whatever would I do if the witch got hold of you and turned you perhaps into blue birds or green frogs, or something dreadful? Whatever *would* your dear papa say to me? Oh, Miss Maia, do tell Master Rollo never to go there again.'

'Don't be afraid,' said Maia; 'we'll take care of ourselves. I can quite promise you we won't be turned into frogs or birds. But don't talk any more about it to-night, Nanni. I'm *so* sleepy, and I don't want to dream of horrible witches.'

And this was all the satisfaction Nanni could get.

But the next morning Rollo and Maia had a grand consultation together. They did not like the idea of not going to the cottage again, for they felt it would not be right not to explain about the milk, and they had besides a motive, which Nanni's strange story had no way lessened-that of great curiosity.

'It would be a shame not to pay for the milk,' said Rollo. 'I should feel uncomfortable whenever I thought of it.'

'So should I,' said Maia; 'even more than you, for it was I that drank it! And I do *so* want to find out who lives there. There *must* be children, I am sure, because of the little beds and chairs and cups, and everything.'

'If they are all for children, I don't know what there is for big people,' said Rollo. 'Perhaps they're some kind of dwarfs that live there.'

'Oh, what fun!' said Maia, clapping her hands. 'Oh, we *must* go back to find out!'

She started, for just as she said the words a voice behind them was heard to say, 'Go back; go back where, my children?'

They were walking up and down the terrace on one side of the castle, where Mademoiselle Delphine had sent them for a little fresh air between their lessons, and they were so engrossed by what they were talking of that they had not heard nor seen the old doctor approaching them. It was his voice that made Maia start. Both children looked rather frightened when they saw who it was, and that he had overheard what they were saying.

'Go back where?' he repeated. 'What are you talking about?'

The children still hesitated.

'We don't like to tell you, sir,' said Rollo frankly. 'You would say it was only fancy, as you did last night, and we *know* it wasn't fancy.'

'Oh, about the cottage?' said the old doctor coolly. 'You needn't be afraid to tell me about it, fancy or no fancy. Fancy isn't a bad thing sometimes.'

'But it *wasn't* fancy,' said both together; 'only we don't like to talk about it for fear of vexing our cousin, and we don't like to go back there without leave, and yet we *should* go back.'

'Why should you?' asked their old friend.

Then Maia explained about the milk, adding, too, the strange things that Nanni had heard in the servants' hall. The old doctor listened attentively. His face looked quite pleased and good-humoured, and yet they saw he was not at all inclined to laugh at them. When they had finished, to the children's surprise he said nothing, but drew out a letter from his pocket.

'Do you know this writing?' he said.

Rollo and Maia exclaimed eagerly, 'Oh, yes; it is our father's. Do you know him? Do you know our father, Mr. Doctor?'

'I have known him,' said the old man, quietly drawing the contents out of the cover, 'I have known him since he was much smaller than either of you is now. It was by my advice he sent you here for a time, and see what he gave me for you.'

He held up as he spoke a small folded paper, which had been inside the other letter. It bore the words: 'For Rollo and Maia-to be given them when you think well.' 'I think well now,' he went on, 'so read what he says, my children.'

They quickly opened the paper. There was not much written inside-just a few words:

'Dear children,' they were, 'if you are in any difficulty, ask the advice of my dear old friend and adviser, the doctor, and you may be sure you will do what will please your father.'

For a moment or two the children were almost too surprised to speak. It was Rollo who found his voice first.

'Give us your advice now, Mr. Doctor. May we go back to the cottage without saying any more about it to Lady Venelda?'

'Yes,' said the old doctor. 'You may go anywhere you like in the woods. No harm will come to you. It is no use your saying any more about the cottage to Lady Venelda. She cannot understand it because she cannot find it. If you can find it you will learn no harm there, and your father would be quite pleased for you to go.'

'Then do you think we may go soon again?' asked the children eagerly.

'You will always have a holiday once a week,' said the doctor. 'It would not be good for you to go *too* often. Work cheerfully and well when you are at work, my children. I will see that you have your play.'

CHAPTER IV
FAIRY HOUSEKEEPING.

> 'Neat, like bees, as sweet and busy,
> . . . . . .
> Aired and set to rights the house;
> Kneaded cakes of whitest wheat —
>
> Cakes for dainty mouths to eat.'

Goblin Market.

The next few days passed rather slowly for the children. There was no talk of another expedition to the woods. And they had a good many lessons to do, so that short walks in the grounds close round the castle were all they had time for. They only saw the old doctor at meal-times, but he always smiled at them, as if to assure them he was not forgetting them, and to encourage them to patience.

There was one person who certainly did not regret the children's not returning to the woods, and that person was Nanni. What she had heard from the servants about the mysterious cottage had thoroughly frightened her; she felt sure that if they went there again something dreadful would happen to them, and yet she was so devoted to them that, however terrified, she would never have thought of not following them wherever they chose to go. But, as day after day went by, and no more was said about it, she began to breathe freely. Her distress was therefore the greater when, one afternoon just six days after the last ramble, Rollo and Maia rushed upstairs after their lessons in the wildest spirits.

'Hurrah for the doctor!' shouted Rollo, and Maia was on the point of joining him, till she remembered that if they made such a noise Lady Venelda would be sending up to know what was the matter.

'We're to have a whole holiday to-morrow, Nanni,' they explained, 'and we're going to spend it in the woods. You're to come with us, and carry something in a basket for us to eat.'

'Very well, Miss Maia,' replied Nanni, prudently refraining from mentioning the cottage, in hopes that they had forgotten about it, 'that will be very nice, especially if it is a fine day, but if not, of course you would not go.'

'I don't know that,' said Rollo mischievously; 'green frogs don't mind rain.'

'Nor blue birds,' added Maia. 'They could fly away if they did.'

At these fateful words poor Nanni grew deadly pale. 'Oh, my children,' she cried; 'oh, Master Rollo and Miss Maia, don't, I beg of you, joke about such things. And oh, I entreat you, don't go looking for that witch's cottage. Unless you promise me you won't, I shall have to go and tell my Lady, however angry she is!'

'No such thing, my good girl,' said a voice at the door. 'You needn't trouble your head about such nonsense. Rollo and Maia will go nowhere where they can get any harm. I know everything about the woods better than you or those silly servants downstairs. Lady Venelda would only tell you not to interfere with what didn't concern you if you went saying anything to her. Go off to the woods with your little master and mistress without misgiving, my good girl, and if the air makes you sleepy don't be afraid to take a nap. No harm will come to you or the children.'

Nanni stood still in astonishment-the tears in her eyes and her mouth wide open, staring at the old doctor, for it was he, of course, who had followed the children upstairs and overheard her remonstrances. She looked so comical that Rollo and Maia could scarcely help laughing at her, as at last she found voice to speak.

'Of course if the learned doctor approves I have nothing to say,' she said submissively; though she could not help adding, 'and I only hope no harm will come of it.'

Rollo and Maia flew to the doctor.

'Oh, that's right!' they exclaimed. 'We are so glad you have spoken to that stupid Nanni. She believes all the rubbish the servants here speak.'

The doctor turned to Nanni again.

'Don't be afraid,' he repeated. 'All will be right, you will see. But take my advice, do not say anything to the servants here about the amusements of your little master and mistress. Least said soonest mended. It would annoy Lady Venelda for it to be supposed they were allowed to go where any harm could befall them.'

'Very well, sir,' replied Nanni, meekly enough, though she still looked rather depressed. She could not help remembering that before he left, old Marc, too, had warned her against too much chattering.

The next morning broke fine and bright. The children started in the greatest spirits, which even Nanni, laden with a basket of provisions for their dinner, could not altogether resist. And before they went, Lady Venelda called them into her boudoir, and kissing them, wished them a happy holiday.

'It's all that nice old doctor,' said Maia. 'You see, Rollo, she hasn't told us not to go to the cottage-he's put it all right, I'm sure.'

'Yes, I expect so,' Rollo agreed; and then in a minute or two he added: 'Do you know, Maia, though of course I don't believe in witches turning people into green frogs, or any of that nonsense, I do think there's *something* funny about that cottage.'

'What sort of something? What do you mean?' asked Maia, looking intensely interested. 'Do you mean something to do with fairies?'

'I don't know —I'm not sure. But we'll see,' said Rollo.

'If we can find it!' said Maia.

'I'm *sure* we shall find it. It's just because of that that I think there's something queer. It must be true that some people can't find it.'

'Naughty people?' asked Maia apprehensively. 'For you know, Rollo, we're not always *quite* good.'

'No, I don't mean naughty people. I mean more people who don't care about fairies and wood-spirits, and things like that-people who call all that nonsense and rubbish.'

'I see,' said Maia; 'perhaps you're right, Rollo. Well, any way, that won't stop *us* finding it, for we certainly do care *dreadfully* about fairy things, don't we, Rollo? But what about Nanni?' she went on, for Nanni was some steps behind, and had not heard what they were saying.

'Oh, as to Nanni,' said Rollo coolly, 'I shouldn't wonder if she took a nap again, as the old doctor said. Any way, she can't interfere with us after *his* giving us leave to go wherever we liked.'

They stopped a little to give Nanni time to come up to them, and Rollo offered to help her to carry the basket. It was not heavy, she replied, she could carry it quite well alone, but she still looked rather depressed in spirits, so the children walked beside her, talking merrily of the dinner in the woods they were going to have, so that by degrees Nanni forgot her fears of the mysterious cottage, and thought no more about it.

It was even a more beautiful day than the one, now nearly a week ago, on which they had first visited the woods. There was more sunshine to-day, and the season was every day farther advancing; the lovely little new green tips were beginning to peep out among the darker green which had already stood the wear and tear of a bitter winter and many a frosty blast.

'How pretty the fir-trees look!' said Maia. 'They don't seem the least dim or gloomy in the sunshine, even though it only gets to them in little bits. See there, Rollo,' she exclaimed, pointing to one which got more than its share of the capricious gilding. 'Doesn't it look like a *real* Christmas-tree?'

'Like a lighted-up one, you mean,' said Rollo. 'It would be a very nice Christmas-tree for a family of giants, and if I could climb up so high, I'd be just about the right size for the angel at the top. Let's spread our table at the foot of this tree-it looks so nice and dry. I'm sure, Nanni,' he went on, 'you'll be glad to get rid of your basket.'

'It's not heavy, Master Rollo,' said Nanni; 'but, all the same, it *is* queer how the minute I get into these woods I begin to be so sleepy-you'd hardly believe it.'

Rollo and Maia looked at each other with a smile, but they said nothing.

'We'd better have our dinner any way,' observed Rollo, kneeling down to unfasten the basket, of which the contents proved very good indeed.

'What fun it is, isn't it?' said Maia, when they had eaten nearly as much cold chicken and bread, and cakes and fruit as they wanted. 'What fun it is to be able to do just as we like, and say just what we like, instead of having to sit straight up in our chairs like two dolls, and only speak when we're spoken to, and all that-how nice it would be if we could have our dinner in the woods every day!'

'We'd get tired of it after a while, I expect,' said Rollo. 'It wouldn't be nice in cold weather, or if it rained.'

'*I* wouldn't mind,' said Maia. 'I'd build a warm little hut and cover it over with moss. We'd live like the squirrels.'

'How do you know how the squirrels live?' said Rollo.

But Maia did not answer him. Her ideas by this time were off on another flight-the thought of a little hut had reminded her of the cottage.

'I want to go farther into the wood,' she said, jumping up. 'Come, Rollo, let's go and explore a little. Nanni, you can stay here and pack up the basket again, can't you?'

'Then you won't be long, Miss Maia,' began Nanni, rather dolefully. 'You won't — —'

'We won't get turned into green frogs, if that's what you're thinking of, Nanni,' interrupted Rollo. 'Do remember what the old doctor said, and don't worry yourself. We shall come to no harm. And as you're so sleepy, why shouldn't you take a nap as you did the other day? Perhaps you'll dream of the beautiful lady again.'

Nanni looked but half convinced.

'It's not *my* fault, any way,' she said. 'I've done all I could. I may as well stay here, for I know you like better to wander about by yourselves. But I'm not going to sleep-you needn't laugh, Master Rollo, I've brought my knitting with me on purpose,' and she drew out a half stocking and ball of worsted with great satisfaction.

The children set off. They were not sure in what direction lay the cottage, for they had got confused in their directions, but they had a vague idea that by continuing upwards, for they were still on sloping ground, they would come to the level space where they had seen the smoke of the burning leaves. They were not mistaken, for they had walked but a very few minutes when the ground ceased to ascend, and looking round they felt sure that they recognised the look of the trees near the cottage.

'This way, Rollo, I am sure,' said Maia, darting forward. She was right-in another moment they came out of the woods just at the side of the cottage. It looked just the same as before, except that no fire was burning outside, and instead, a thin column of smoke rose gently from the little chimney. The gate of the little garden was also open, as if inviting them to enter.

'They must be at home, whoever they are,' said Rollo. 'There is a fire in the kitchen, you see, Maia.'

Maia grew rather pale. Now that they were actually on the spot, she began to feel afraid, though of what she scarcely knew. Nanni's queer hints came back to her mind, and she caught hold of Rollo's arm, trembling.

'Oh, Rollo,' she exclaimed, 'suppose it's true? About the witch, I mean-or suppose they have found out about the milk and are very angry?'

'Well, we can't help it if they are,' replied Rollo sturdily. 'We've done the best thing we could in coming back to pay for it. You've got the little purse, Maia?'

'Oh, yes, it's safe in my pocket,' she said. 'But — —'

She stopped, for just at that moment the door of the cottage opened and a figure came forward. It was no 'old witch,' no ogre or goblin, but a young girl —a little older than Maia she seemed-who stood there with a sweet, though rather grave expression on her face and in her soft dark eyes, as she said gently, 'Welcome-we have been expecting you.'

'Expecting us?' exclaimed Maia, who generally found her voice more quickly than Rollo; 'how can you have been expecting us?'

She had stepped forward a step or two before her brother, and now stood looking up in the girl's face with wonder in her bright blue eyes, while she tossed back the long fair curls that fell round her head. Boys are not very observant, but Rollo could not help noticing the pretty picture the two made. The peasant maiden with her dark plaits and brown complexion, dressed in a short red skirt, and little loose white bodice fastened round the waist with a leather belt, and Maia with a rather primly-cut frock and frilled tippet of flowered chintz, such as children then often wore, and large flapping shady hat.

'How can you have been expecting us?' Maia repeated.

Rollo came forward in great curiosity to hear the answer.

The girl smiled.

'Ah!' she said, 'there are more ways than one of knowing many things that are to come. Waldo heard you had arrived at the white castle, and my godmother had already told us of you. Then we found the milk gone, and — —'

Rollo interrupted this time. 'We were so vexed,' he said, 'not to be able to explain about it. We have wanted to come every day since to — —' 'To pay for it,' he was going to say, but something in the girl's face made him hesitate.

'Not to pay for it,' she said quickly, though smiling again, as if she read his words in his face; 'don't say that. We were so glad it was there for you. Besides, it is not ours-Waldo and I would have nothing but for our godmother. But come in-come in-Waldo is only gone to fetch some brushwood, and our godmother, too, will be here soon.'

Too surprised to ask questions-indeed, there seemed so many to ask that they would not have known where to begin-Rollo and Maia followed the girl into the little kitchen. It looked just as neat and dainty as the other day-and brighter too, for a charming little fire was burning in the grate, and a pleasant smell of freshly-roasted coffee was faintly perceived. The table was set out as before, but with the addition of a plate of crisp-looking little cakes or biscuits, and in place of *two* small cups and saucers there were *four*, as well as the larger one the children had seen before. This was too much for Maia to behold in silence. She stopped short, and stared in still greater amazement.

'Why!' she exclaimed. 'You don't mean to say-why, just fancy, I don't even know your name.'

'Silva,' replied the girl quietly, but with an amused little smile on her face.

'Silva,' continued Maia, 'you *don't* mean to say that you've put out those two cups for *us* —that you knew we'd come.'

'Godmother did,' said Silva. 'She told us yesterday. So we've been very busy to get all our work done, and have a nice holiday afternoon. Waldo has nothing more to do after he's brought in the wood, and I baked those little cakes this morning and roasted the coffee. Godmother told us to have it ready early, so that there'll be plenty of time before you have to go. Oh, here's Waldo!' she exclaimed joyfully.

Rollo and Maia turned round. There, in the doorway stood a boy, his cap in his hand, a pleasant smile on his bright ruddy face.

'Welcome, my friends,' he said, with a kind of gravity despite his smile.

He was such a nice-looking boy-just about as much bigger than Rollo as Silva was bigger than Maia. You could have told at once that they were brother and sister-there was the same bright and yet serious expression in their eyes; the same healthy, ruddy complexion; the same erect carriage and careless grace in Waldo in his forester's clothes as in Silva with her pretty though simple peasant maiden dress. They looked what they were, true children of the beautiful woods.

'Thank you,' said Rollo and Maia, after a moment's hesitation. They did not know what else to say. Silva glanced at them. She seemed to have a curious power of reading in their faces the thoughts that were passing in their minds.

'Don't think it strange,' she said quickly, 'that Waldo calls you thus "my friends," and that we both speak to you as if we had known you for long. We know we are not the same as you-in the world, I mean, we could not be as we are here with you, but this is not the world,' and here she smiled again-the strange, bright, and yet somehow rather sad smile which made her face so sweet —'and so we need not think about it. Godmother said it was best only to remember that we are just four children together, and when you see her you will feel that what she says is always best.'

'We don't need to see her to feel that we like you to call us your friends,' exclaimed Rollo and Maia together. The words came from their hearts, and yet somehow they felt surprised at being able to say them so readily. Rollo held out his hand to Waldo, who shook it heartily, and little Maia going close up to Silva said softly, 'Kiss me, please, dear Silva.'

And thus the friendship was begun.

The first effect of this seemed to be the setting loose of Maia's tongue.

'There are so many things I want to ask you,' she began. 'May I? Do you and Waldo live here alone, and have you always lived here? And does your godmother live here, for the other day when we went all over the cottage we only saw two little beds, and two little of everything, except the big chair and the big cup and saucer. And what — —'

Here Rollo interrupted her.

'Maia,' he said, 'you really shouldn't talk so fast. Silva could not answer all those questions at once if she wanted; and perhaps she doesn't want to answer them all. It's rude to ask so much.'

Maia looked up innocently into Silva's face.

'I didn't mean to be rude,' she said, 'only you see I can't help wondering.'

'We don't mind your asking anything you like,' Silva replied. 'But I don't think I *can* tell you all you want to know. You'll get to see for yourself. Waldo and I have lived here a long time, but not *always*!'

'But your godmother,' went on Maia; 'I do so want to know about her. Does *she* live here? Is it she that the people about call a witch?' Maia lowered her voice a little at the last word, and looked up at Rollo apprehensively. Would not he think speaking of witches still ruder than asking questions? But Silva did not seem to mind.

'I dare say they do,' she said quietly. 'They don't know her, you see. I don't think she would care if they did call her a witch. But now the coffee is ready,' for she had been going on with her preparations meanwhile, 'will you sit round the table?'

'We are not very hungry,' said Rollo, 'for we had our dinner in the wood. But the coffee smells so good,' and he drew in his chair as he spoke. Maia, however, hesitated.

'Would it not be more polite, perhaps,' she said to Silva, 'to wait a little for your godmother? You said she would be coming soon.'

'She doesn't like us to wait for her,' said Silva. 'We always put her place ready, for sometimes she comes and sometimes she doesn't —we never know. But she says it is best just to go on regularly, and then we need not lose any time.'

'I don't think I should like that way,' said Maia. 'Would you, Rollo? If father was coming to see us, I would like to know it quite settledly ever so long before, and plan all about it.'

'But it isn't quite the same,' said Silva. 'Your father is far away. Our godmother is never very far away-it is just a nice feeling that she may come any time, like the sunshine or the wind.'

'Well, perhaps it is,' said Maia. 'I dare say I shall understand when I've seen her. How very good this coffee is, Silva, and the little cakes! Did your godmother teach you to make them so nice?'

'Not exactly,' said Silva; 'but she made me like doing things well. She made me see how pretty it is to do things rightly —*quite* rightly, just as they should be.'

'And do you always do things that way?' exclaimed Maia, very much impressed. '*I* don't; I'm very often dreadfully untidy, and sometimes my exercise-books are full of blots and mistakes. I wish I had had your godmother to teach me, Silva.'

'Well, you're going to have her now. She teaches without one knowing it. But *I'm* not perfect, nor is Waldo! Indeed we're not-and if we thought we were it would show we weren't.'

'Besides,' said Waldo, 'all the things we have to do are very simple and easy. We don't know anything about the world, and all we should have to do and learn if we lived there.'

'Should you like to live there?' asked Maia. Both Waldo and Silva hesitated. Then both, with the grave expression in their eyes that came there sometimes, replied, 'I don't know;' but Waldo in a moment or two added, 'If it had to be, it would be right to like it.'

'Yes,' said Silva quietly. But something in their tone made both Rollo and Maia feel puzzled. 'I do believe you're both half fairies,' exclaimed Maia with a little impatience; 'I can't make you out at all.'

Rollo felt the same, though, being more considerate than his little sister, he did not like to express his feelings so freely. But Waldo and Silva only laughed merrily.

'No, no, indeed we're not,' they said more than once, but Maia did not seem convinced by any means, and she was going on to maintain that no children who *weren't* half fairies could live like that by themselves and manage everything so beautifully, when a slight noise at the door and a sudden look of pleasure on Silva's face made her stop short and look round.

'Here she is,' exclaimed Waldo and Silva together. 'Oh, godmother, darling, we are so glad. And they have come, Rollo and Maia have come, just as you said.'

And thus saying they sprang forward. Their godmother stooped and kissed both on the forehead.

'Dear children,' she said, and then she turned to the two strangers, who were gazing at her with all their eyes.

'*Can* it be she the silly people about call a witch?' Maia was saying to herself. 'It *might* be, and yet I don't know. *Could* any one call her a witch?'

She was old-of that there was no doubt, at least so it seemed at the first glance. Her hair was perfectly white, her face was very pale. But her eyes were the most wonderful thing about her. Maia could not tell what colour they were. They seemed to change with every word she said, with every new look that came over her face. Old as she was they were very bright and beautiful, very soft and sweet too, though not the sort of eyes-Maia said afterwards to Rollo —'that I would like to look at me if I had been naughty.' Godmother was not tall; when she first came into the little kitchen she seemed to stoop a little, and did not look much bigger than Silva. And she was all covered over with a dark green cloak, almost the colour of the darkest of the foliage of the fir-trees.

'One would hardly see her if she were walking about the woods,' thought Maia, 'except that her face and hair are so white, they would gleam out like snow.'

CHAPTER V
THE STORY OF A KING'S DAUGHTER.

'Gentle and sweet is she;
As the heart of a rose is her heart,

As soft and as fair and as sweet.'

Liliput Lectures.

Godmother turned to the little strangers. The two pairs of blue eyes were still fixed upon her. *Her* eyes looked very kind and gentle, and yet very 'seeing', as she caught their gaze.

'I believe,' thought Maia, 'that she can tell all we are thinking;' and Rollo had something of the same idea, yet neither of them felt the least afraid of her.

'Rollo and Maia, dear children, too,' she said, 'we are so pleased to see you.'

'And we are very pleased to be here,' said they; 'but ——' and then they hesitated.

'You are puzzled how it is I know your names, and all about you, are you not?' she said, smiling. 'I puzzle most children at first; but isn't it rather nice to be puzzled?'

This was a new idea. Thinking it over, they began to find there was something in it.

'I think it *is*,' both replied, smiling a little.

'If you knew all about everything, and could see through everything, there wouldn't be much interest left. Nothing to find out or to fancy. Oh, what a dull world!'

'Are we to find out or to fancy *you?*' asked Maia. She spoke seriously, but there was a little look of fun in her eyes which was at once reflected in godmother's.

'Whichever you like,' she replied; 'but, first of all, you are to kiss me.'

Rollo and Maia both kissed the soft white face. It was *so* soft, and there seemed a sort of fresh, sweet scent about godmother, as if she had been in a room all filled with violets, only it was even nicer. She smiled, and from a little basket on her arm, which they had not noticed, she drew out several tiny bunches of spring flowers, tied with green and white ribbon-so pretty; oh, so very pretty!

'So you scented my flowers,' she said. 'No wonder; you have never scented any quite like them before. They come from the other country. Here, dears, catch,' and she tossed them up in the air, all four children jumping and darting about to see who would get most. But at the end, when they counted their treasures, it was quite right, each had got three.

'Oh, how sweet!' cried Maia. 'May we take them home with us, godmother?' It seemed to come quite naturally to call her that, and Maia did it without thinking.

'Certainly,' godmother replied; 'but remember this, don't throw them away when they seem withered. They will not be really withered; that is to say, long afterwards, by putting them in the sunshine, they will-some of them, any way-come out quite fresh again. And even when dried up they will have a delicious scent; indeed, the scent has an added charm about it the older they are-so many think, and I agree with them.'

Rollo and Maia looked at their flowers with a sort of awe.

'Then they are *fairy* flowers?' they half whispered. 'You said they came from the other country. Do you come from there too, godmother? Are you a fairy?'

Godmother smiled.

'Fancy me one if you like,' she said. 'Fancy me whatever you like best, you will not be far wrong; but fairyland is only one little part of that other country. You will find that out as you get older.'

'Shall we go there some day, then?' exclaimed Maia. 'Will you take us, dear godmother? Have Waldo and Silva ever been?'

'Oh, what a lot of questions all at once!' cried godmother. 'I can't answer so many. You must be content to find out some things for yourself, my little girl. The way to the other country for one. Shall you go there some day? Yes, indeed, many and many a time, I hope.'

Maia clapped her hands with delight.

'Oh, how nice!' she said. 'And when? May we go to-day? Oh, Silva, do ask godmother to let us go to-day,' she exclaimed, catching hold of Silva in her eagerness. But Silva only smiled, and looked at godmother; and somehow, when they smiled, the two faces-the young one with its bright rich colour, and the old one, white, so white, except for the wonderful, beautiful eyes, that it might have been made of snow-looked strangely alike.

'Silva has learned to be patient,' said godmother, 'and so she gets to know more and more of the other country. You must follow her example, little Maia. Don't be discouraged. How do you know that you are not already on the way there? What do you think about it, my boy?' she went on, turning to Rollo, who was standing a little behind them listening, but saying nothing.

Rollo looked up and smiled.

'I'd like to find the way myself,' he replied.

'That's right,' said godmother. And Maia felt more and more puzzled, as it seemed to her that Rollo understood the meaning of godmother's words better than she did.

'Rollo,' she exclaimed, half reproachfully.

Rollo turned to her with some surprise.

'You understand and I don't,' she said, with a little pout on her pretty lips.

'No,' said Rollo, 'I don't. But I like to think of understanding some day.'

'That is right,' said godmother again. 'But this is dull talk for you, little people. What is it to be to-day, Silva? What is old godmother to do for you?'

Silva glanced out of the window.

'The day will soon be closing into evening,' she said,' and Rollo and Maia cannot stay after sunset. We have not very long, godmother-no time to go anywhere.'

'Ah, I don't know about that,' godmother replied. 'But still-the first visit. What would you like, then, my child?'

'Let us gather round the fire, for it is a little chilly,' said Silva, 'and you, dear godmother, will tell us a story.'

Maia's eyes and Rollo's, too, brightened at this. Godmother had no need to ask if they would like it. She drew the large chair nearer the fireplace, and the four children clustered round her in silence waiting for her to begin.

'It is too warm with my cloak on,' she said, and she raised her hand to unfasten it at the neck and loosen it a little. It did not entirely fall off; the dark green hood still made a shade round her silvery hair and delicate face, but the cloak dropped away enough for Maia's sharp eyes to see that the dress underneath was of lovely crimson stuff, neither velvet nor satin, but richer and softer than either. It glimmered in the light of the fire with a sort of changing brilliance that was very tempting, and it almost seemed to Maia that she caught the sparkle of diamonds and other precious stones.

'May I stroke your pretty dress, godmother?' she said softly. Godmother started; she did not seem to have noticed how much of the crimson was seen, and for a moment Maia felt a little afraid. But then godmother smiled again, and the child felt quite happy, and slipped her hand inside the folds of the cloak till it reached the soft stuff beneath.

'Stroke it the right way,' said godmother.

'Oh, how soft!' said Maia in delight. 'What is it made of? It isn't velvet, or even plush. Godmother,' she went on, puckering her forehead again in perplexity, 'it almost feels like *feathers*. Are you perhaps a *bird* as well as a fairy?'

At this godmother laughed. You never heard anything so pretty as her laugh. It was something like-no, I could never tell you what it was like —a very little like lots of tiny silver bells ringing, and soft breezes blowing, and larks trilling, all together and *very* gently, and yet very clearly. The children could not help all laughing, too, to hear it.

'Call me whatever you like,' said godmother. 'A bird, or a fairy, or a will-o'-the-wisp, or even a witch. Many people have called me a witch, and I don't mind. Only, dears,' and here her pretty, sweet voice grew grave, and even a little sad, 'never think of me except as loving you and wanting to make you happy and good. And never believe I have said or done anything to turn you from doing right and helping others to do it. That is the only thing that could grieve me. And the world is full of people who don't see things the right way, and blame others when it is their own fault all the while. So sometimes you will find it all rather difficult. But don't forget.'

'No,' said Maia, 'we won't forget, even though we don't quite understand. We will some day, won't we?'

'Yes, dears, that you will,' said godmother.

'And just now,' said Silva, 'it doesn't matter. We needn't think about the difficult world, dear godmother, while we're *here* —ever so far away from it.'

'No, we need not,' said godmother, with what sounded almost like a sigh, if one could have believed that godmother *could* sigh! If it were one, it was gone in an instant, and with her very prettiest and happiest smile, godmother turned to the children.

'And now, dears,' she said, 'now for the story.'

The four figures drew still nearer, the four pair of eyes were fixed on the sweet white face, into which, as she spoke, a little soft pink colour began to come. Whether it was from the reflection of the fire or not, Maia could not decide, and godmother's clear voice went on.

'Once —— '

'Once upon a time; do say "once upon a time,"' interrupted Silva.

'Well, well, once upon a time,' repeated godmother, 'though, by the by, how do you know I was *not* going to say it? Well, then, once upon a time, a long ago once upon a time, there lived a king's daughter.'

'A princess,' interrupted another voice, Maia's this time. 'Why don't you say a princess, dear godmother?'

'Never mind,' replied godmother. 'I like better to call her a king's daughter.'

'And don't interrupt any more, please,' said Waldo and Rollo together, quite forgetting that they were actually interrupting themselves.

'And,' continued godmother, without noticing this last interruption, 'she was very beautiful and very sweet and good, even though she had everything in the world that even a king's daughter could want. Do you look surprised at my saying "even though," children? You need not; there is nothing more difficult than to remain unselfish, which is just another word for "sweet and good," if one never knows what it is to have a wish ungratified. But so it was with Auréole, for that was the name of the fair maiden. Though she had all her life been surrounded with luxury and indulgence, though she had never known even a crumpled rose-leaf in her path, her heart still remained tender, and she felt for the sufferings of others whenever she knew of them, as if they were her own.

'"Who knows?" she would say softly to herself, "who knows but what some day sorrow may come to me, and then how glad I should be to find kindness and sympathy!"

'And when she thought thus there used to come a look in her eyes which made her old nurse, who loved her dearly, tremble and cross herself.

'"I have never seen that look," she would whisper, though not so that Auréole could hear it —"I have never seen that look save in the eyes of those who were born to sorrow."

'But time went on, and no sorrows of her own had as yet come to Auréole. She grew to be tall and slender, with golden fair curls about her face, which gave her a childlike, innocent look, as if she were younger than her real age. And with her years her tenderness and sympathy for suffering seemed to grow deeper and stronger. It was the sure way to her heart. In a glade not far from the castle she had a favourite bower, where early every morning she used to go to feed and tend her pets, of which the best-loved was a delicate little fawn that she had found one day in the forest, deserted by its companions, as it had hurt its foot and could no longer keep pace with them. With difficulty Auréole and her nurse carried it home between them, and tended it till it grew well again and could once more run and spring as lightly as ever. And then one morning Auréole, with tears in her eyes, led it back to the forest where she had found it.

"'Here, my fawn,' she said, "you are free as air. I would not keep you a captive. Hasten to your friends, my fawn, but do not forget Auréole, and if you are in trouble come to her to help you."

'But the fawn would not move. He rubbed himself softly against her, and looked up in her face with eyes that almost spoke. She could not but understand what he meant to say.

"'I cannot leave you. Let me stay always beside you,' was what he tried to express. So Auréole let him follow her home again, and from that day he had always lived in her bower, and was never so happy as when gambolling about her. She had other pets too-numbers of birds of various kinds, none of which she kept in cages, for all of them she had in some way or other saved and protected, and, like the fawn, they refused to leave her. The sweetest, perhaps, were a pair of wood-pigeons which she had one day released from a fowler's snare, where they had become entangled. It was the prettiest sight in the world to see Auréole in her bower every morning, the fawn rubbing his soft head against her white dress, and the wood-pigeons cooing to her, one perched on each shoulder, while round her head fluttered a crowd of birds of different kinds-all owing their life and happiness to her tender care. There was a thrush, which she had found half-fledged and gasping for breath, fallen from the nest; a maimed swallow, who had been left behind by his companions in the winter flight. And running about, though still lame of one leg, a tame rabbit which she had rescued from a dog, and ever so many other innocent creatures, all with histories of the same kind, and each vying with the other to express gratitude to their dear mistress as she stood there with the sunshine peeping through the boughs and lighting up her sweet face and bright hair.

'It was the prettiest sight in the world to see Auréole in her bower every morning.'

'But summer and sunshine do not always last, and in time sorrow came to Auréole as to others.

'Her mother had died when she was a little baby, and her father was already growing old. But he felt no anxiety about the future of his only child, for it had long been decided that she was to marry the next heir to his crown, the Prince Halbert, as by the laws of that country no woman could reign. Auréole had not seen Halbert for many years, when, as children, they had played together; but she remembered him with affection as a bright merry boy, and she looked forward without fear to being his wife.

"'Why should I not love him?" she said to herself. "I have never yet known any one who was not kind and gentle, and Halbert will be still more so to me than any one else, for he will be my king and master."

'And when the day came for the Prince to return to see her again, she waited for him quietly and without misgiving. And at first all seemed as she had pictured it. Halbert was manly and handsome, he had an open expression and winning manners, he was devoted to his gentle cousin. So the old King was delighted, and Auréole said to herself, "What have I done to deserve such happiness? How can I ever sufficiently show my gratitude?"

'She was standing in her bower when she thought thus, surrounded as usual by her pets. Suddenly among the trees at some little distance she heard a sound of footsteps, and at the same time a harsh voice, which she scarcely recognised, speaking roughly and sharply.

"'Out of my way, you cur," it said, and then came the sound of a blow, followed by a piteous whine.

'Auréole darted forward, and in another instant came upon Halbert, his face dark and frowning, while a poor little dog lay bleeding at his feet.

"'Halbert!" exclaimed Auréole. Her cousin started; he had not heard her come. "Did *you* do this? Did *you* strike the little dog?"

'Halbert turned towards her; he had reddened with shame, but he tried to laugh it off.

"'It is nothing," he said; "the creature will be all right again directly. Horrid little cur! it rushed out at me from that cottage there and yelped and barked just when I was eagerly hastening to your bower, Princess."

'But Auréole hardly heard him, or his attempts at excusing himself. She was on her knees before the poor dog.

"'Why, Fido," she said, "dear little Fido, do you not know me?" Fido feebly tried to wag his tail.

"'Is it *your* dog?" stammered Halbert. "I had no-not the slightest idea ——"

'But Auréole flashed back an answer which startled him. "*My* dog," she said. "No. But what has that to do with it? Oh, you cruel man!"

'Then she turned from him, the little dog all panting and bleeding in her arms. Halbert was startled by the look on her face.

"'Forgive me, Auréole," he cried. "I did not mean to hurt the creature. I am hasty and quick-tempered, but you should not punish so severely an instant's thoughtlessness."

"'It was not thoughtlessness. It was cowardly cruelty," replied Auréole slowly, turning her pale face towards him. "A man must have a cruel nature who, even under irritation, could do what you have done. Farewell," and she was moving away when he stopped her.

"'What do you mean by farewell? You are not in earnest?" he exclaimed. But Auréole looked at him with indignation.

"'Not in earnest?" she repeated. "Never was I more so in my life! Farewell, Halbert."

"'And you will not see me again?" he exclaimed.

"'I will never see you again," Auréole replied, "till you have learnt to feel for the sufferings of your fellow-creatures, instead of adding to them. And who can say if that day will ever come? Farewell again, Halbert."

'The Prince stood thunderstruck, watching her slight figure as it disappeared among the trees. He felt like a man in a dream. Then, as he gradually became conscious that it was all true, his hot temper broke out in anger at Auréole, in mockery at her absurdity and exaggeration, and he tried to believe what he said, that no man could be happy with so fanciful and unreasonable a wife, and that he had nothing to regret. In his heart he was angry with himself, though to this he would not own, and conscious also that Auréole's instinct had judged him truly. He was selfish and utterly thoughtless for others, and far on the way therefore to becoming actually cruel. He had, like Auréole, been surrounded by luxury and indulgence all his life, but had not, like her, acquired the habit of feeling for others and looking upon his own blessings as to be shared with those who were without them.

'Auréole kept to her word. She would not see Halbert again, though the King, her father, did his utmost to shake her resolution. She remained firm. It was better so for both of them, she repeated. It would kill her to be the wife of such a man, and do him no good. So in bitter and angry resentment, rather than sorrow, Prince Halbert went away, and Auréole's life returned to what it had been before his coming.

CHAPTER VI
THE STORY OF A KING'S DAUGHTER

(Continued).

'I have been enchanted, and thou only

canst set me free.'

GRIMM'S *Raven.*

'It seemed so at least, but in reality it was very different. Auréole had received a shock which she felt deeply, and which she could not forget. It grieved her, too, to see her father's distress and disappointment, and sometimes she asked herself if perhaps she had done wrong in deciding so hastily. But the sight of the little dog Fido, which had recovered, though with the loss of one eye, always removed these misgivings. "A man who could be so cruel to a harmless little creature, would have quickly broken my heart," she said to herself and sometimes to her father. And as time went on, and news came that Prince Halbert was becoming more and more feared and disliked in his own home from the increasing violence of his temper, the old King learnt to be thankful that his dear Auréole was not to be at the mercy of such a man.

'"But what will become of you, my darling, when I am gone?" he would say.

'"Fear not for me," Auréole assured him. "I have no fear for myself, father, dear. Why, I could live safely in the woods with my dear animals. If I had a little hut, and Fido to guard me, and Lello my fawn, and the little rabbit, and all my pretty birds, I should be quite happy!"

'For the forester to whom Fido belonged had begged Auréole to keep him, as even before its hurt the dog had learnt to love her and spring out to greet her, and wag his tail with pleasure when she passed his master's cottage, which lay on the way to her glade. But though Auréole was not afraid for herself, she was often very miserable when she thought of her country-people, above all the poor and defenceless ones, in the power of such a king as Halbert gave signs of being, after the long and gentle rule of her father. Yet there was nothing to be done, so she kept silence, fearing to cloud with more sorrow and anxiety the last days of the old King.

'They were indeed his last days, for within a year of Halbert's unfortunate visit her father died, and the fair Auréole was left desolate.

'Her grief was great, even though the King had been very old, and she had long known he could not be spared to her for many more years. But she had not much time to indulge in it, for already, before her father was laid in his grave, her sorrow was disturbed by the strange and unexpected events which came to pass.

'These began by a curious dream which came to Auréole the very night of her father's death.

'She dreamt that she was standing in her bower with her pets about her as usual. She felt bright and happy, and had altogether forgotten about her father's death. Suddenly a movement of terror made itself felt among her animals-the birds fluttered closer to her, the little rabbit crept beneath her skirt, the fawn and Fido looked up at her with startled eyes, and almost before she had time to look round their terror was explained. A frightful sound was heard approaching them, the terrible growl of a bear, and in another moment the monster was within a few yards. Even then, in her dream, Auréole's first thought was for her pets. She threw her arms round all that she could embrace, and stood there calmly, watching the creature with a faint hope that if she showed no terror he might pass them by. But he came nearer and nearer, till she almost felt his hot breath on her face, when suddenly, to her amazement, the monster was no longer there, but in his place the Prince Halbert, standing beside her and looking at her with an expression of the profoundest misery.

"'I have brought it on myself," he said. "I deserve it; but pity me, oh, Auréole! Sweet Auréole, pity and forgive me!" Then a cry of irrepressible grief burst from his lips, and at this moment Auréole awoke, to find her eyes wet with tears, her heart throbbing fast with fear and distress.

"'What can have made me dream of Halbert?" she said to herself. "It must have been seeing the messengers start yesterday," and then all came back to her memory, which at the first moment of waking had been confused, and she remembered her father's death and her own loneliness, and the scarcely-dried tears rushed afresh to her eyes.

"'Has any news come from Prince Halbert?" she inquired of her attendants when they came at her summons. And when they told her "none," she felt a strange sensation of uneasiness. For the messengers had been despatched at once on the death of the old King, which had been sudden at the last, to summon his successor, and there had been time already for their return.

'And as the day went on and nothing was heard of them, every one began to think there must be something wrong, till late at night these fears were confirmed by the return of the messengers with anxious faces.

"'Has the Prince arrived?" was their first question, and when they were told that nothing had been seen of him, they explained the reason of their inquiry.

'Halbert, already informed of the illness of the old King, had quickly prepared to set out with his own attendants and those who had come to summon him. They had ridden through the night, and had nothing untoward occurred, they would have ended their journey by daybreak. But the Prince had lost his temper with his horse, a nervous and restless animal, unfit for so irritable a person to manage.

"'We became uneasy," said the messengers, "on seeing the Prince lashing and spurring furiously the poor animal, who, his sides streaming with blood, no longer understood what was required of him, and at last, driven mad with pain and terror, dashed off at a frantic pace which it was hopeless to overtake. We followed him as best we could, guided for some distance by the branches broken as they passed and the ploughed-up ground, which, thanks to a brilliant moonlight, we were able to distinguish. But at last, where the trees began to grow more thickly — —" and here the speaker, who was giving this report to Auréole herself, hesitated —"at last these traces entirely disappeared. We sought on in every direction; when the moon went in we waited for the daylight, and resumed our search. But all to no purpose, and at last we resolved to ride on hither, hoping that the Prince might possibly have found his way before us."

"'But this is terrible!" cried Auréole, forgetting all her indignation against Halbert in the thought of his lying perhaps crushed and helpless in some bypath of the forest which his followers had missed. "We must at once send out fresh horsemen in every direction to scour the country."

'The captain who had had command of the little troop bowed, but said nothing, and seemed without much hope that any fresh efforts would succeed. Auréole was struck with his manner.

"'You are concealing something from me," she said. "Why do you appear so hopeless? Even at the worst, even supposing the Prince is killed, he must be found."

"'We searched too thoroughly," replied the officer. "Wherever it was *possible* to get, we left not a square yard unvisited."

"'Wherever it was *possible*," repeated Auréole; "what do you mean? You do not think — —" and she too hesitated, and her pale face grew paler.

'The captain glanced at her.

"'I see that you have divined our fears, Princess," he said in a low voice. "Yes, we feel almost without a doubt that the unfortunate Prince has been carried into the enchanted forest, from whence, as you well know, none have ever been known to return. It is well that his parents have not lived to see this day, for, though he brought it on himself, it is impossible not to feel pity for such a fate."

'Auréole seemed scarcely able to reply. But she gave orders, notwithstanding all she had heard, to send out fresh horsemen to search again in every direction.

"'My poor father," she said to herself; "I am glad he was spared this new sorrow about Halbert." And as the remembrance of her strange dream returned to her, "Poor Halbert," she added, "what may he not be suffering?" and she shuddered at the thought.

'For the enchanted forest was the terror of all that country. In reality nothing, or almost nothing, was known of it, and therefore the awe and horror about it were the greater. It lay in a lonely stretch of ground between two ranges of hills, and no one ever passed through it, for there was no pathway or entrance of any kind to be seen. But for longer than any one now living could remember, it had been spoken of as a place to be dreaded and avoided, and travellers in passing by used to tell how they had heard shrieks and screams and groans from among its dark shades. It was said that a magician lived in a castle in the very centre of the forest, and that he used all sorts of tricks to get people into his power, whence they could never again escape. For though several were known to have been tempted to enter the forest, none of them were ever heard of or seen again. And it was the common saying of the neighbourhood, that it would be far worse to lose a child by straying into the forest than by dying. No one had ever seen the magician, no one even was sure that he existed, but when any misfortune came over the neighbourhood, such as a bad harvest or unusual sickness, people were sure to say that the wizard of the forest was at the bottom of it. And Auréole, like every one else, had a great and mysterious terror of the place and its master.

"'Poor Halbert!" she repeated to herself many times that day. "Would I could do anything for him!"

'The bands of horsemen she had sent out returned one after the other with the same tidings, —nothing had been seen or heard of the Prince. But late in the day a woodman brought to the castle a fragment of cloth which was recognised as having been torn from the mantle of the Prince, and which he had found caught on the branch of a tree. When asked where, he hesitated, which of itself was answer enough.

"'Close to the borders of the enchanted forest," he said at last, lowering his voice. But that was all he had to tell. And from this moment all lost hope. There was nothing more to be done.

"'The Prince is as lost to us as is our good old King," were the words of every one on the day of the funeral of Auréole's father. "Far better for him were he too sleeping peacefully among his fathers than to be where he is."

'It seemed as if it would have certainly been better for his people had it been so. It was impossible to receive the successor of Halbert as king till a certain time had elapsed, which would be considered as equal to proof of his death. And the next heir to the crown being but an infant living in a distant country, the delay gave opportunity for several rival claimants to begin to make difficulties, and not many months after the death of the old King the once happy and peaceful country was threatened with war and invasion on various sides. Then the heads of the nation consulted together, and decided on a bold step. They came to Auréole offering her the crown, declaring that they preferred to overthrow the laws of the country, though they had existed for many centuries, and to make her, at the point of the sword if necessary, their queen, rather than accept as sovereign any of those who had no right to it, or an infant who would but be a name and no reality.

'Auréole was startled and bewildered, but firm in her refusal.

"'A king's daughter am I, but no queen. I feel no fitness for the task of ruling," she replied, "and I could never rest satisfied that I was where I had a right to be."

'But when the deputies entreated her to consider the matter, and when she thought of the misery in store for the people unless something were quickly done, she agreed to think it over till the next day.

'The next day came, Auréole was ready, awaiting the deputies. Their hopes rose high as they saw her, for there was an expression on her face that had not been there the day before. She stood before them in her long mourning robe, but she had encircled her waist with a golden belt, and golden ornaments shone on her neck and arms.

"'It is a good sign,' the envoys whispered, as they remarked also the bright and hopeful light in her eyes, and they stood breathless, waiting for her reply. It was not what they had expected.

"'I cannot as yet consent to what you wish,' said Auréole; "but be patient. I set off to-day on a journey from which I hope to return with good news. Till then I entreat you to do your best to keep all peaceful and quiet. And I promise you that if I fail in what I am undertaking, I will return to be your queen."

'This was all she would say. She was forbidden, she declared, to say more. And so resolute and decided did she appear, that the envoys, though not without murmuring, were obliged to consent to await her return, and withdrew with anxious and uneasy looks.

'And Auréole immediately began to get ready for the mysterious journey of which she had spoken. Her preparations were strange. She took off, for the first time since her father's death, her black dress, and clad herself entirely in white. Then she kissed her old nurse and bade her farewell, at the same time telling her to keep up her courage and have no fear, to which the old dame could not reply without tears.

"'I do not urge you to tell me the whole, Princess,' she said, "as it was forbidden you to do so. But if I might but go with you." Auréole shook her head.

"'No, dear nurse,' she replied. "The voice in my dream said, 'Alone, save for thy dumb friends.' That is all I can tell you," and kissing again the poor nurse, Auréole set off, none knew whither, and she took care that none should follow her. Some of her attendants saw her going in the direction of her bower, and remarked her white dress. But they were so used to her going alone to see her pets that they thought no more of it. For no one knew the summons Auréole had received. The night before, after tossing about unable to sleep, so troubled was she by the request that had been made to her, she at last fell into a slumber, and again there came to her a strange dream. She thought she saw her cousin; he seemed pale and worn with distress and suffering.

"'Auréole,' he said, "you alone can rescue me. Have you courage? I ask it not only for myself, but for our people."

'And when in her sleep she would have spoken, no words came, only she felt herself stretching out her arms to Halbert as if to reach and save him.

"'Come, then,' said his voice; "but come alone, save for thy dumb friends. Tell no one, but fear not." But even as he said the words he seemed to disappear, and again the dreadful, the panting roar she had heard in her former dream reached Auréole's ears, in another moment the terrible shape of the monster appeared, and shivering with horror she awoke. Yet she determined to respond to Halbert's appeal. She told no one except her old nurse, to whom she merely said that she had been summoned in a dream to go away, but that no harm would befall her. She clad herself in white, as a better omen of success, and when she reached her bower, all her creatures welcomed her joyfully. So, with Fido, Lello the fawn, and the little rabbit gambolling about her feet, the wood-pigeons on her shoulders, and all the strange company of birds fluttering about her, Auréole set off on her journey, she knew not whither.

'But her pets knew. Whenever she felt at a loss Fido would give a little tug to her dress and then run on barking in front, or Lello would look up in her face with his pleading eyes and then turn his head in a certain direction, while the birds would sometimes disappear for a few moments and then, with a great chirping and fluttering, would be seen again a little way overhead, as if to assure her they had been to look if she was taking the right way. So that when night began to fall, Auréole, very tired, but not discouraged, found herself far from home in a part of the forest she had never seen before, though with trembling she said to herself that for all she knew she might already be in the enchanter's country.

"'But what if it be so?' she reflected. "I must not be faint-hearted before my task is begun."

'She was wondering how she should spend the night when a sharp bark from Fido made her look round. She followed to where it came from, and found the little dog at the door of a small hut cleverly concealed among the trees. Followed by her pets Auréole entered it, when immediately, as if pulled by an invisible hand, the door shut to. But she forgot to be frightened in her surprise at what she saw. The hut was beautifully made of the branches of trees woven together, and completely lined with moss. A small fire burned cheerfully in one corner, for the nights were still chilly; a little table was spread with a snow-white cloth, on which were laid out fruits and cakes and a jug of fresh milk; and a couch of the softest moss covered with a rug made of fur was evidently arranged for Auréole's bed. And at the other side of the hut sweet hay was strewn for the animals, and a sort of trellis work of branches was ready in one corner for the birds to roost on.

"How pleasant it is!" said Auréole, as she knelt down to warm herself before the fire. "If this is the enchanted forest I don't think it is at all a dreadful place, and the wizard must be very kind and hospitable."

'And when she had had some supper and had seen that her pets had all they wanted, she lay down on the mossy couch feeling refreshed and hopeful, and soon fell fast asleep. She had slept for some hours when she suddenly awoke, though what had awakened her she could not tell. But glancing round the hut, by the flickering light of the fire, which was not yet quite out, she saw that all her pets were awake, and when she gently called "Fido, Fido," the little dog, followed by the fawn and the rabbit, crept across the hut to her, and when she touched them she felt that they were all shaking and trembling, while the birds seemed to be trying to hide themselves all huddled together in a corner. And almost before Auréole had time to ask herself what it could be, their fear was explained, for through the darkness outside came the sound she had twice heard in her dreams-the terrible panting roar of the monster! It came nearer and nearer. Auréole felt there was nothing to do. She threw her arms round the poor little trembling creatures determined to protect them to the last. Suddenly there came a great bang at the door, as if some heavy creature had thrown itself against it, and Auréole trembled still more, expecting the door to burst open. But the mysterious hand that had shut it had shut it well. It did not move. Only a low despairing growl was heard, and then all was silent till a few minutes after, when another growl came from some distance off, and then Auréole felt sure the danger was past: the beast had gone away, for, though she had not seen him, she was certain he was none other than the monster of her dreams. The poor animals cowered down again in their corner, and Auréole, surprised at the quickness with which her terror had passed, threw herself on her couch and fell into a sweet sleep. When she woke, the sun was already some way up in the sky; the door was half open, and a soft sweet breeze fluttered into the hut. All was in order; the little fire freshly lighted, the remains of last night's supper removed, and a tempting little breakfast arranged. Auréole could scarcely believe her eyes. "Some one must have come in while I was asleep," she said, and Fido seemed to understand what she meant. He jumped up, wagging his tail, and was delighted when Auréole sat down at the little table to eat what was provided. All her pets seemed as happy as possible, and had quite forgotten their fright. So, after breakfast, Auréole called them all about her and set off again on her rambles. Whither she was to go she knew not; she had obeyed the summons as well as she could, and now waited to see what more to do. The animals seemed to think they had got to the end of their journey, and gambolled and fluttered about in the best of spirits. And even Auréole herself felt it impossible to be sad or anxious. Never had she seen anything so beautiful as the forest, with its countless paths among the trees, each more tempting than the other, the sunshine peeping in through the branches, the lovely flowers of colours and forms she had never seen before, the beautiful birds warbling among the trees, the little squirrels and rabbits playing about, and the graceful deer one now and then caught sight of.

"Why," exclaimed Auréole, "*this* the terrible enchanted forest! It is a perfect fairyland."

"You say true," said a voice beside her, which made her start. "To such as *you* it is a fairyland of delight. But to *me*!" and before Auréole could recover herself from her surprise, there before her stood the Prince Halbert! But how changed! Scarcely had she recognised him when every feeling was lost in that of pity.

"Oh, poor Halbert," she cried, "so I have found you! Where have you been? What makes you look so miserable and ill?"

'For Halbert seemed wasted to a shadow. His clothes, torn and tattered, hung loosely about him. His face was pale and thin, and his eyes sad and hopeless, though, as he saw the pitying look in her face, a gleam of brightness came into his.

"'Oh, Auréole, how good of you to come! It is out of pity for *me*, who so little deserve it. But will you have strength to do all that is required to free me from this terrible bondage?"

"'Explain yourself, Halbert," Auréole replied. "What is it you mean? What bondage? Remember I know nothing; not even if this is truly the enchanted forest."

'Halbert glanced at the sun, now risen high in the heavens. "I have but a quarter of an hour," he said. "It is only one hour before noon that I am free."

'And then he went on to relate as quickly as he could what had come over him. Fallen into the power of the invisible spirits of the enchanted land, whose wrath he had for long incurred by his cruelty to those beneath him, among whom were poor little Fido, and the unhappy horse who had dropped dead beneath him as soon as they entered the forest, his punishment had been pronounced to him by a voice in his dreams. It was a terrible one. For twenty-three hours of the twenty-four which make the day and night, he was condemned to roam the woods in the guise of a dreadful monster, bringing terror wherever he came. "I have to be in appearance what I was formerly in heart," he said bitterly. "You cannot imagine how fearful it is to see the tender innocent little animals fleeing from me in terror, though I would now die rather than injure one of them. And even you, Auréole, if you saw me you too would rush from me in horror."

"'I have seen you," she replied. "I have twice seen you in my dreams, and now that I know all I shall not fear you."

"'Do you indeed think so?" he exclaimed eagerly. "Your pity and courage are my only hope. For I am doomed to continue this awful life-for hundreds of years perhaps-till twelve dumb animals mount on my back and let me carry them out of this forest. In my despair, when I heard this sentence, I thought of you and your favourites, whom I used to mock at and ill-treat more than you knew. They love and trust you so much that it is possible you may make them do this. But I fear for your own courage."

"'No," said Auréole, "that will not fail. And Fido is of a most forgiving nature. See here," she went on, calling to the little dog, "here is poor Halbert, who wants you to love him. Stroke him, Halbert," and as the Prince gently did so, Fido looked up in his face with wistful eyes, and began timidly to wag his tail, while Lello and the rabbit drew near, and the birds fluttered, chirping above their heads. It was a pretty picture.

"'See," said Auréole, raising her bright face from caressing the good little creatures, "see, Halbert, how loving and gentle they are! It will not be difficult. In many ways they are wiser than we. But I can never again believe that the spirits of the forest are evil or mischievous. Rather do I now think them good and benevolent. How happy seem all the creatures under their care!"

"'I know no more than I have told you," said Halbert; "but I too believe they must be good, cruelly as they have punished me, for I deserved it. And doubtless all those who are said to have disappeared in the forest have been kept here for good purposes. And such as you, Auréole, have nothing to fear in any country or from any spirits. But I must go," he exclaimed, "I would not have you *yet* see me in my other form. You must reflect over what I have said, and prepare yourself for it."

"'And when, then, shall I see you again?" she asked.

"'To-night, at sunset, at the door of your hut, you will see-alas, not *me*!" he whispered, and then in a moment he had disappeared.

'At sunset that evening Auréole sat at the door of the little hut, surrounded by her animals. She had petted and caressed them even more than usual, so anxious was she to prepare them for their strange task. She had even talked of it to Fido and Lello with a sort of vague idea that they might understand a little, though their only answer was for Fido to wag his tail and

Lello to rub his soft nose against her. But suddenly both pricked up their ears, and then clinging more closely to their mistress, began to tremble with fear, while the birds drew near in
a frightened flock.

"'Silly birds," said Auréole, trying to speak in her usual cheerful tone, "what have *you* to
fear? Bears don't eat little birds, and you can fly off in a moment. Not that I want you to fly
away;" and she whistled and called to them, at the same time caressing and encouraging the
animals, whose quick ears had caught sooner than she had done the dreadful baying roar which
now came nearer and nearer. It was exactly the scene of her dreams, and notwithstanding all
her determination, Auréole could not help shivering as the form of the monster came in sight.
"Suppose it is not Halbert," she thought. "Suppose it is all a trick of the spirits of this enchanted
country for my destruction!" And the idea nearly made her faint as the dreadful beast drew near.
He was so hideous, and his roars made him seem still more so. His great red tongue hung out
of his mouth, his eyes seemed glaring with rage. It was all Auréole could do to keep her pets
round her, and she felt that her terror would take away all her power over them.

Auréole could not help shivering as the form of the monster came in sight.

"'Oh, Halbert," she exclaimed, "*is* it you? I know you cannot speak, but can you not make
some sign to show me that it is you? I am so frightened." She had started up as if on the

point of running away. The monster, who was close beside her, opened still wider his huge mouth, and gave a roar of despair. Then an idea seemed to strike him-he bent his clumsy knees, and rubbed his great head on the ground at her feet; Auréole's courage returned. She patted his head, and he gave a faint groan of relief. Then by degrees, with the greatest patience, she coaxed the animals to draw near, and at last placed Fido and Lello on the beast's immense back. But though they now seemed less frightened they would not stay there, but jumped off again, and pressed themselves close against her. It was no use; after hours, at least so it seemed to Auréole, spent in trying, she had to give it up.

"'I cannot do it, Halbert," she said. A groan was his reply. Then another thought struck her.

"'I will climb on your back myself," she exclaimed; "and then perhaps I can coax the animals to stay there."

'The poor beast tried to stoop down still lower to make it easier for Auréole to get on. She managed it without much difficulty, and immediately Fido and Lello and the rabbit saw her mounted, up they jumped, for they had no idea of being left behind. The wood-pigeons came cooing down from the branch where they had taken refuge in their fright, and perched on her shoulders. Auréole looked up, and called and whistled to the other birds. Down they came as if bewitched, and settled round her, all the seven of them on the beast's furry back.

"'Off, Halbert," cried Auréole, afraid to lose an instant, and off, nothing loth, the beast set. It was hard work to keep on. He plunged along so clumsily, and went so fast in his eagerness, that it was like riding on an earthquake. But when now and then he stopped, and gave a low pitiful roar, as if begging Auréole's pardon for shaking her so, she always found breath to say: "On, Halbert, on; think not of me."

'And so at last, after hours of this terrible journey, many times during which Auréole's heart had been in her mouth at the least sign of impatience among the animals, they reached the borders of the enchanted country, and as the panting beast emerged from the forest with his strange burden, poor Auréole slipped fainting off his back. Her task was done.

'When she came back to her senses and opened her eyes, her first thought was for the beast, but he had disappeared. Fido and Lello, and all the others were there, however; the dog licking her hands, the fawn nestling beside her, and at a little distance stood a figure she seemed to know, though no longer miserable and wretched as she had last seen him. It was Halbert, strong and handsome and happy again, but with a look in his eyes of gentleness and humility and gratitude that had never been there in the old days.

"'Halbert," said Auréole, sitting up and holding out her hand to him, "is all then right?"

"'All is right," he replied; "you can see for yourself. But, oh, Auréole, how can I thank you? My whole life would not be long enough to repay or —— "

"'Think not about thanking me," interrupted Auréole. "My best reward will be the delight of restoring to my dear country-people a king whose first object will *now*, I feel assured, be their happiness;" and her eyes sparkled with delight at the thought.

'She was right. Nothing could exceed the joy of the nation at the return of Auréole, and thanks to her assurances of his changed character, they soon learned to trust their new king as he deserved.

'No one ever knew the true history of his disappearance, but all admired and respected the noble and unselfish courage of Auréole in braving the dangers of the enchanted forest itself. Her pets all lived to a good old age, and had every comfort they could wish for. It was said that Halbert's only sorrow was that for long he could not persuade Auréole to fulfil her father's wishes by marrying him. But some years later a rumour came from the far-off country where these events happened, telling of the beautiful "king's daughter" having at last consented to become a king's wife as well, now that she knew Halbert to be worthy of her fullest affection.

'And if this is true, I have no doubt it was for their happiness as well as for that of their subjects, among whom I include the twelve faithful animals.'

CHAPTER VII
A WINDING STAIR AND A SCAMPER.

> 'But children, to whom all is play,
>   And something new each hour must bring,
> Find everything so strange, that they
>
> Are not surprised at anything.'

> *The Fairies' Nest.*

Godmother's voice stopped. For a moment or two there was silence.

'I hope it *was* true,' said Maia, the first to find her tongue. 'Poor Halbert, I think he deserved to be happy at the end. I think Auréole was rather-rather —*cross*, don't you, Silva?'

Silva considered. 'No,' she said. 'I can't bear people that are cruel to little animals. Oh!' and she clasped her hands, 'if only Rollo and Maia could see some of our friends in the wood! May they not, godmother?'

'All in good time,' said godmother, rather mysteriously.

Maia looked at her. 'Godmother,' she said, 'how funny you are! I believe you like puzzling people better than anything. There are such a lot of things I want to ask you about the story. Who was it lived in the forest? *Was* it a wizard? I think that would be much nicer than invisible spirits, even though it is rather frightening. And who was it made Auréole's breakfast and shut the door, and all that? I am sure you know, godmother. I believe you've been in the enchanted forest yourself. *Have* you?'

Godmother smiled. 'Perhaps,' she said. But when Maia went on questioning, she would not say any more. 'Keep something to puzzle about,' she said. 'Remember that that is half the pleasure.'

And then she took Maia up on her knee and gave her such a sweet kiss that the child could not grumble.

'You are *very* funny, godmother,' she repeated.

Suddenly Rollo started.

'Maia,' he exclaimed, 'I am afraid we are forgetting about going home and meeting Nanni and everything. It must be getting very late. It is so queer,' he added with a sigh, glancing round the dear little kitchen, 'I seemed to have forgotten that *this* isn't our home, and yet we have only been here an hour or two, and — —'

'Yes,' said Maia, 'I feel just the same. Indeed Auréole and her pets seem far more real to me now than Lady Venelda and the white castle.'

'And the old doctor and all the lessons you have to do,' said godmother; and somehow the children no longer felt surprised at her knowing all about everything. 'But you are right, my boy, good boy,' she went on, turning to Rollo. 'There is a time for all things, and now it is time to go back to your other life. Say good-bye to each other, my children,' and when they had done so-very reluctantly, you may be sure-she took Rollo by one hand and Maia by the other, Waldo and Silva standing at the cottage-door to see them off, and led them across the little clearing, away into the now darkening alleys of the wood.

'Are you going with us to where Nanni is?' asked Maia.

'Not to where you left her. I will take you by a short cut,' said godmother, who, since they had left the cottage, had seemed to grow into just an ordinary-looking old peasant woman, very bent and small, for any one at least who did not peep far enough inside her queer hood to see her wonderful eyes and gleaming hair, and whom no one would have suspected of the marvellous crimson dress under the long dark cloak. Maia kept peeping up at her with a strange look in her face.

'What is it, my child?' said godmother.

'I don't quite know,' Maia replied. 'I'm not quite sure, godmother, if I'm not a little —a very little-frightened of you. You change so. In the cottage you seemed a sort of a young fairy godmother-and now — —' she hesitated.

'And now do I seem very old?'

'*Rather*,' said Maia.

'Well, listen now. I'll tell you the real truth, strange as it may seem. I am *very* old-older than you can even fancy, and yet I am and I always shall be young.'

'In fairyland-in the other country, do you mean?' asked Rollo.

Godmother turned her bright eyes full upon him. 'Not only there, my boy,' she said. 'Here, too-everywhere —I am both old and young.'

Maia gave a little sigh.

'You are very nice, godmother,' she said, 'but you are *very* puzzling.' But she had no time to say more, for just then godmother stopped.

'See, children,' she said, pointing down a little path among the trees, 'I have brought you a short cut, as I said I would. At the end of that alley you will find your faithful Nanni. And that will not be the end of the short cut. Twenty paces straight on in the same direction you will come out of the wood. Cross the little bridge across the brook and you will only have to climb a tiny hill to find yourselves at the back entrance of the castle. All will be right-and now good-bye, my dears, till your next holiday. Have you your flowers?'

'Oh, yes,' exclaimed both, holding up the pretty bunches as they spoke; 'but how are we to — —'

'Don't trouble about how you are to see me again,' she interrupted, smiling. 'It will come-you will see,' and then before they had time to wonder any more, she turned from them, waving her hand in farewell, and disappeared.

'Rollo,' said Maia, rubbing her eyes as if she had just awakened, 'Rollo, is it all *real*? Don't you feel as if you had been dreaming?'

'No,' said Rollo. 'I feel as if *it*' —and he nodded his head backwards in the direction of the cottage —'were all real, and the castle and our cousin and Nanni and all *not* real. You said so too.'

'Yes,' said Maia meditatively, 'while I was there with them, I felt like that. But now I don't. It seems not real, and I don't want to begin to forget them.'

'Suppose you scent your flowers,' said Rollo; 'perhaps that's why godmother gave them to us.'

Maia thought it a good idea.

'Yes,' she said, poking her little nose as far as it would go in among the fragrant blossoms, 'yes, Rollo, it comes back to me when I scent the flowers. I think it is because godmother's red dress was scented the same way. Oh, yes!' shutting her eyes, 'I can *feel* her soft dress now, and I can hear her voice, and I can see Waldo and Silva and the dear little kitchen. How glad I am you thought of the flowers, Rollo!'

'But we must run on,' said Rollo, and so they did. But they had not run many steps before the substantial figure of Nanni appeared; she was looking very comfortable and contented.

'You have not stayed very long, Master Rollo and Miss Maia,' she said, 'but I suppose it is getting time to be turning home.'

'And have you spent a pleasant afternoon, Nanni?' asked Rollo quietly. 'How many stockings have you knitted?'

'How many!' repeated Nanni; 'come, Master Rollo, you're joking. You've not been gone more than an hour at the most, but it is queer-it must be the smell of the fir-trees —as soon as ever I sit down in this wood, off I go to sleep! I hadn't done more than two rounds when my head began nodding, so I had to put my knitting away for fear of running the needles into my eyes. And I had such pleasant dreams.'

'About the beautiful lady again?' asked Maia.

'I think so, but I can't be sure,' said Nanni. 'It was about all sorts of pretty things mixed up together. Flowers and birds, and I don't know what. And the flowers smelt, for all the world, just like the roses round the windows of my mother's little cottage at home. I could have believed I was there.'

Rollo and Maia looked at each other. It was all godmother's doing, they felt sure. How clever of her to know just what Nanni would like to dream of.

By this time they were out of the wood. The light was brighter than among the trees, but still it was easy to see that more than Nanni's 'hour' must have passed since they left her.

'Dear me,' she exclaimed, growing rather frightened, 'it looks later than I thought! And we've a long way to go yet,' she went on, looking round; 'indeed,' and her rosy face grew pale, 'I don't seem to know exactly where we are. We must have come another way out of the wood-oh, dear, dear ——'

'Don't get into such a fright, Nanni,' said Rollo; 'follow me.'

He sprang up the hilly path that godmother had told them of, Maia and Nanni following. It turned and twisted about a little, but when they got to the top, there, close before them, gleamed the white walls of the castle, and a few steps more brought them to a back entrance to the terrace by which they often came out and in.

'Well, to be sure!' exclaimed Nanni, 'you are a clever boy, Master Rollo. Who ever would have guessed there was such a short cut, and indeed I can't make it out at all which way we've come back. But so long as we're here all in good time, and no fear of a scolding, I'm sure I'm only too pleased, however we've got here.'

As they were passing along the terrace the old doctor met them.

'Have you had a pleasant holiday?' he asked.

'Oh, *very*,' answered both Rollo and Maia, looking up in his face, where, as they expected, they saw the half-mysterious, half-playful expression they had learnt to know, and which seemed to tell that their old friend understood much more than he chose to say.

'Did you find any pretty flowers?' he asked, with a smile, 'though it is rather early in the year yet-especially for scented ones-is it not?'

'But we *have* got some,' said Maia quickly, and glancing round to see if Nanni were still by them. She had gone on, so Maia drew out her bunch, and held them up. '*Aren't* they sweet?' she said.

The old man pressed them to his face almost as lovingly as Maia herself. 'Ah, how *very* sweet!' he murmured. 'How much they bring back! Cherish them, my child. You know how?'

'Yes, *she* told us,' said Maia. 'You know whom I mean, don't you, Mr. Doctor?'

The old doctor smiled again. Maia drew two or three flowers out of her bunch, and Rollo did the same. Then they put them together and offered them to their old friend.

'Thank you, my children,' he said; 'I shall add the thought of you to many others, when I perceive their sweet scent.'

'And even when they're withered and dried up, Mr. Doctor, you know,' said Maia eagerly, 'the scent, *she* says, is even sweeter.'

'I know,' said the doctor, nodding his head. 'Sweeter, I truly think, but bringing sadness with it too; very often, alas!' he added in a lower voice, so low that the children could not clearly catch the words.

'We must go in, Maia,' said Rollo; 'it must be nearly supper-time.'

'Yes,' said Maia; 'but first, Mr. Doctor, I want to know when are we to have another holiday? Lady Venelda will do any way you tell her, you know.'

'All in good time,' replied the doctor, at which Maia pouted a little.

'I don't like all in good time,' she said.

'But you have never known me to forget,' said the old doctor.

'No, indeed,' said Rollo eagerly, and then Maia looked a little ashamed of herself, and ran off smiling and waving her hand to the doctor.

Lady Venelda asked them no questions, and made no remarks beyond saying she was glad they had had so fine a day for their ramble in the woods. She seemed quite pleased so long as the children were well and sat up straight in their chairs without speaking at meal-times, and there were no complaints from their teachers. That was the way *she* had been brought up, and she thought it had answered very well in her case. But she was really kind, and the children no longer felt so lonely or dull, now that they had the visits to the wood to look forward to. Indeed, they had brought back with them a fund of amusement, for now their favourite play was to act the story which godmother had told them, and as they had no other pets, they managed to make friends with the castle cat, a very dignified person, who had to play the parts of Fido and Lello and the rabbit all in one; while the birds were represented by bunches of feathers they picked up in the poultry-yard, and the great furry rug with which they had travelled turned Rollo into the unhappy monster. It was very amusing, but after a few days they began to wish for other companions.

'If Silva and Waldo were here,' said Rollo, 'what fun we could have! I wonder what they do all day, Maia.'

'They work pretty hard, I fancy,' said Maia. 'Waldo goes to cut down trees in the forest a good way off, I know, and Silva has all the house to take care of, and everything to cook and wash, and all that. But *I* should call that play-work, not like lessons.'

'And *I* should think cutting down trees the best fun in the world,' said Rollo. 'That kind of work can't be as tiring as lessons.'

'Lessons, lessons! What is all this talk about lessons? Are you so terribly overworked, my poor children? What should you say to a ramble in the woods with me for a change?' said a voice beside them, which made the children start.

It was the doctor. He had come round the corner of the wall without their seeing him, for they were playing on the terrace for half an hour between their French lesson with Mademoiselle and their history with the chaplain.

'A walk with you, Mr. Doctor!' exclaimed Maia. 'Oh, yes, it *would* be nice. But it isn't a holiday, and ——'

'How do *you* know it isn't a holiday, my dear young lady,' interrupted the doctor. 'How do you know that I have not represented to your respected cousin that her young charges had been working very hard of late, and would be the better for a ramble? If you cannot believe me, run in and ask Lady Venelda herself; if you are satisfied without doing so, why then, let us start at once!'

'Of course we are satisfied,' exclaimed Rollo and Maia together; 'but we must go in to get our thick boots and jackets, and our nicer hats,' added Maia, preparing to start off.

'Not a bit of it,' said the doctor, stopping her. 'You are quite right as you are. Come along;' and without giving the children time for even another 'but,' off he strode.

To their amazement, however, he turned towards the house, which he entered by a side door that the children had never before noticed, and which he opened with a small key.

'Doctor,' began Maia, but he only shook his head without speaking, and stalked on, Rollo and his sister following. He led them some way along a rather narrow passage, where they had never been before, then, opening a door, signed to them to pass in in front of him, and when they had done so, he too came in, and shut the door behind him. It was a queer little room–the doctor's study evidently, for one end was completely filled with books, and at one side, through the glass doors of high cupboards in the wall, all kinds of mysterious instruments, chemical tubes and globes, high bottles filled with different-coloured liquids, and ever so many things the children had but time to glance at, were to be perceived. But the doctor had evidently not brought them there to pay him a visit. He touched a spring at the side of the book-shelves, and a small door opened.

'Come, children,' he said, speaking at last, 'this is another short cut. Have no fear, but follow me.'

Full of curiosity, Rollo and Maia pressed forward. The doctor had already disappeared–all but his head, that is to say–for a winding staircase led downwards from the little door, and Rollo first, then Maia, were soon following their old friend step by step, holding by one hand to a thick cord which supplied the place of a handrail. It was almost quite dark, but they were not frightened. They had perfect trust in the old doctor, and all they had seen and heard since they came to the white castle had increased their love of adventure, without lessening their courage.

'Dear me,' said Maia, after a while, for it was never easy for her to keep silent for very long together, 'it isn't a *very* short cut! We seem to have been going down and down for a good while. My head is beginning to feel rather turning with going round and round so often. How much farther are we to go before we come out, Mr. Doctor?'

But there was no answer, only a slight exclamation from Rollo just in front of her, and then all of a sudden a rush of light into the darkness made Maia blink her eyes and for a moment shut them to escape the dazzling rays.

'Good-bye,' said a voice which she knew to be the doctor's; 'I hope you will enjoy yourselves.'

Maia opened her eyes. She had felt Rollo take her hand and draw her forwards a little. She opened her eyes, but half shut them again in astonishment.

'*Rollo!*' she exclaimed.

'And you said it was not much of a short cut,' replied Rollo, laughing.

No wonder Maia was astonished. They were standing a few paces from the cottage door! The sun was shining brightly on the little garden and peeping through the trees, just in front of which the children found themselves.

'Where have we come from?' said Maia, looking round her confusedly.

'Out of here, I think,' said Rollo, tapping the trunk of a great tree close beside him. 'I think we must have come out of a door hidden in this tree.'

'But we kept coming *down*,' said Maia.

'At first; but the last part of the time it seemed to me we were going up; we must have come down the inside of the hill and then climbed up a little way into the tree.'

'Oh, I am sure we weren't going *up*,' said Maia. 'I certainly was getting quite giddy with going round and round, but I'm *sure* I could have told if we'd been going up.'

'Well, never mind. If godmother is a witch, I fancy the doctor's a wizard. But any way we're here, and that's the principal thing. Come on, quick, Maia, aren't you in a hurry to know if Waldo and Silva are at home?'

He ran on to the cottage and Maia after him. The door was shut. Rollo knocked, but there was no answer.

'Oh, what a pity it will be if they are not in!' said Maia. 'Knock again, Rollo, louder.'

Rollo did so. Still there was no answer.

'What shall we do?' said the children to each other. 'It would be too horrid to have to go home and miss our chance of a holiday.'

'We might stay in the woods by ourselves,' suggested Rollo.

'It would be very dull,' said Maia disconsolately. 'I don't think the old doctor should have brought us without knowing if they would be here. If he knows so much he might have found that out.'

Suddenly Rollo gave an exclamation. He had been standing fumbling at the latch.

'What do you say?' asked Maia.

'The door isn't locked. Suppose we go in? It would be no harm. They weren't a bit vexed with us for having gone in and drunk the milk the first time.'

'Of course not,' said Maia; 'they wouldn't be the least vexed. I quite thought the door was locked all this time. Open it, Rollo. I can't reach so high or I would have found out long ago it wasn't locked.'

With a little difficulty Rollo opened the door.

Everything in the tiny kitchen looked as they had last seen it, only, if that were possible, still neater and cleaner. Maia stared round as if half expecting to see Waldo or Silva jump out from under the chairs or behind the cupboard, but suddenly she darted forward. A white object on the table had caught her attention. It was a sheet of paper, on which was written in round clear letters:

'Godmother will be here in a quarter of an hour.'

'See, Rollo,' exclaimed Maia triumphantly, 'this must be meant for *us*. What a good thing we came in! I don't mind waiting a quarter of an hour.'

'But that paper may have been here all day. It may have been sent for Waldo and Silva,' said Rollo. 'You know they told us godmother only comes sometimes to see them.'

'I don't care,' said Maia, seating herself on one of the high-backed chairs. 'I'm going to wait a quarter of an hour, and just *see*. Godmother doesn't do things like other people, and I'm sure this message is for us.'

Rollo said no more, but followed Maia's example. There they sat, like two little statues, the only distraction being the tick-tack of the clock, and watching the long hand creep slowly down the three divisions of its broad face which showed a quarter of an hour. It seemed a very long quarter of an hour. Maia was so little used to sitting still, except when she was busy with lessons, to which she was obliged to give her attention, that after a few minutes her head began to nod and at last gave such a jerk that she woke up with a start.

'Dear me, isn't it a quarter of an hour *yet*?' she exclaimed.

'No, it's hardly five minutes,' said Rollo, rather grumpily, for he thought this was a very dull way of spending a holiday, and he would rather have gone out into the woods than sit there waiting. Maia leant her head again on the back of her chair.

'Suppose we count ten times up to sixty,' she said. 'That would be ten minutes if we go by the ticks of the clock, and if she isn't here then, I won't ask you to wait any longer.'

'We can see the time,' said Rollo; 'I don't see the use of counting it loud out.'

Maia said nothing more. Whether she took another little nap; whether Rollo himself did not do so also I cannot say. All I know is that just exactly as the hand of the clock had got to fourteen minutes from the time they had begun watching it, both children started to their feet and looked at each other.

'Do you hear?' said Maia.

'It's a carriage,' exclaimed Rollo.

'How could a carriage come through the wood? There's no path wide enough.'

'But it *is* a carriage;' and to settle the point both ran to the door to see.

It came swiftly along, in and out among the trees without difficulty, so small was it. The two tiny piebald ponies that drew it shook their wavy manes as they danced along, the little bells on their necks ringing softly. A funny idea struck Maia as she watched it. It looked just like a toy meant for some giant's child which had dropped off one of the huge Christmas-trees, waiting there to be decked for Santa Claus's festival! But the queerest part of the sight for them was when the carriage came near enough for them to see that godmother herself was driving it. She did look so comical, perched up on the little seat and chirruping and wo-wohing to her steeds, and she seemed to have grown so small, oh, so small! Otherwise how could she ever have got into a carriage really not much too large for a baby of two years old?

On she drove, and drew up in grand style just in front of where the children were standing.

'Jump in,' she said, nodding off-handedly, but without any other greeting.

'But how — —?' began Maia. 'How can Rollo and I possibly get into that tiny carriage?' were the words on her lips, but somehow before she began to say them, they melted away, and almost without knowing how, she found herself getting into the back seat of the little phaeton, with Rollo beside her, and in another moment-crack! went godmother's whip, and off they set.

They went so fast, oh, so fast! There did not seem time to consider whether they were comfortable or not, or how it was they fitted so well into the carriage, small as it was, or anything but just the delicious feeling of flying along, which shows that they must have been very comfortable, does it not? In and out among the great looming pine-trees their strange coachman made her way, without once hesitating or wavering, so that the children felt no fear of striking against the massive trunks, even though it grew darker and gloomier and the Christmas-trees had certainly never looked anything like so enormous.

'Or *can* it be that we have really grown smaller?' thought Maia; but her thoughts were quickly interrupted by a merry cry from godmother, 'Hold fast, children, we're going to have a leap.'

Godmother was certainly in a very comical humour. But for her voice and her bright eyes when they peeped out from under her hood the children would scarcely have known her. She was like a little mischievous old sprite instead of the soft, tender, mysterious being who had petted them so sweetly and told them the quiet story of gentle Auréole the other day. In a different kind of way Maia felt again almost a *very* little bit afraid of her, but Rollo's spirits rose with the fun, his cheeks grew rosier and his eyes brighter, though he was very kind to Maia too, and put his arm round her to keep her steady in preparation for godmother's flying leap, over they knew not what. But it was beautifully managed; not only the ponies, but the carriage too, seemed to acquire wings for the occasion, and there was not the slightest jar or shock, only a strange lifting feeling, and then softly down again, and on, on, through trees and brushwood, faster and faster, as surely no ponies ever galloped before.

'Are you frightened, Rollo?' whispered Maia.

'Not a bit. Why should I be? Godmother can take care of us, and even if she wasn't there, one couldn't be frightened flying along with those splendid little ponies.'

'What was it we jumped over?' asked Maia.

Godmother heard her and turned round.

'We jumped over the brook,' she said. 'Don't you remember the little brook that runs through the wood?'

'The brook that Rollo and I go over by the stepping stones? It's a very little brook, godmother. I should think the carriage might have driven over without jumping.'

'Hush!' said godmother, 'we're getting into the middle of the wood and I must drive carefully.'

But she did not go any more slowly; it got darker and darker as the trees grew more closely together. The children saw, as they looked round, that they had never been so far in the forest before.

'I wonder when we shall see Silva and Waldo,' thought Maia, and somehow the thought seemed to bring its answer, for just as it passed through her mind, a clear bright voice called out from among the trees:

'Godmother, godmother, don't drive too far. Here we are waiting for you.'

'Waldo and Silva!' exclaimed the children. The ponies suddenly stopped, and out jumped or tumbled into the arms of their friends Rollo and Maia.

'Oh, Waldo! oh, Silva!' they exclaimed. 'We've had *such* a drive! Godmother has brought us along like the wind.'

Silva nodded her head. 'I know,' she said, smiling. 'There is no one so funny as godmother when she is in a wild humour. You may be glad you are here all right. She would have thought nothing of driving on to —— ' Silva stopped, at a loss what place to name.

'To where?' said the children.

'Oh, to the moon, or the stars, or down to the bottom of the sea, or anywhere that came into her head!' said Silva, laughing. 'For, you know, she can go *anywhere*.'

'*Can* she?' exclaimed Maia. 'Oh, what wonderful stories we can make her tell us, then! Godmother, godmother, do you hear what Silva says?' she went on, turning round to where she thought the carriage and ponies and godmother were standing. But ——

CHAPTER VIII
THE SQUIRREL FAMILY.

'How extremely pretty!

Won't you jump again?'

Child-World.

—-Godmother was no longer there. She and the carriage and the ponies had completely disappeared. Maia opened her eyes and mouth with amazement, and stood staring. Waldo and Silva and Rollo too could not help bursting out laughing; she looked so funny. Maia felt a little offended.

'I don't see what there is to laugh at,' she said; 'especially for *you*, Rollo. Aren't you astonished too?'

'I don't think I should ever be astonished at anything about godmother,' said Rollo. 'Besides, I saw her drive off while you were kissing Silva. She certainly went like the wind.'

'And where are we?' asked Maia, looking round her for the first time; 'and what are we going to do, Silva?'

'We are going to pay a visit,' said Silva. 'Waldo and I had already promised we would when we got the message that you were coming, so godmother said she would go back and fetch you.'

'But who brought you a message that we were coming?' asked Maia.

'One of godmother's carrier-pigeons. Ah, I forgot, you haven't seen them yet!'

'And *where* are we going?'

'To spend the afternoon with the squirrel family. It's close to here, but we must be quick. They will have been expecting us for some time. You show us the way, Waldo; you know it best.'

It was dark in the wood, but not so dark as it had been when they were driving with godmother, for a few steps brought them out into a little clearing, something like the one where the cottage stood, but smaller. The mossy grass here was particularly beautiful, so bright and green and soft that Maia stooped down to feel it with her hand.

'I suppose no one ever comes this way?' she said. 'Is it because no one ever tramples on it that the moss is so lovely?'

'Nobody but us and the squirrels,' said Silva. 'Sometimes we play with them out here, but to-day we are going to see them in their house. Sometimes they have parties, when they invite their cousins from the other side of the wood. But I don't think any of them are coming to-day.'

Silva spoke so simply that Maia could not think she was making fun of her, and yet it was very odd to speak of squirrels as if they were *people*. Maia could not, however, ask any more, for suddenly Waldo called out:

'Here we are! Silva, you are going too far.'

Rollo and Maia looked round, but they saw nothing except the trees. Waldo was standing just in front of one, and as the others came up to him he tapped gently on the trunk.

'Three times,' said Silva.

'I know,' he replied. Then he tapped twice again, Rollo and Maia looking on with all their eyes. But it was their ears that first gave them notice of an answer to Waldo's summons. A quick pattering sound, like the rush of many little feet, was heard inside the trunk, then with a kind of squeak, as if the hinges were somewhat rusty, a door, so cleverly made that no one could have guessed it was there, for it was covered with bark like the rest of the trunk, slowly opened from the inside, showing a dark hollow about large enough for one child at a time to creep into on hands and knees.

'Who will go first?' said Waldo, lifting his little red cap as he looked at Maia.

'What nice manners he has,' she thought to herself. 'I think you had better go first, please,' she said aloud. For though she would not own it, the appearance of the dark hole rather alarmed her.

'But we can't *all* get in there,' said Rollo.

'Oh, yes,' replied Waldo. 'I'll go first, and when I call out "all right," one of you can come after me. The passage gets wider directly, or–any way there's lots of room–you'll see,' and, ducking down, he crept very cleverly into the hollow, and after a moment his voice was heard, though in rather muffled tones, calling out 'all right.' Rollo, not liking to seem backward, went next, and Maia, who was secretly trembling, was much comforted by hearing him exclaim, 'Oh, how beautiful!' and when Silva asked her to go next, saying 'Maia might like to know she was behind her,' she plunged valiantly into the dark hole. She groped with her hands for a moment or two, till the boys' voices a little way above her led her to a short flight of steps, which she easily climbed up, and then a soft light broke on her eyes, and she understood why Rollo had called out, 'Oh, how beautiful!'

They stood at the entrance of a long passage, quite wide enough for two to walk abreast comfortably. It was entirely lined and carpeted with moss, and the light came from the roof, though *how* one could not tell, for it too was trellised over with another kind of creeping plant, growing too thickly for one to see between. The moss had a sweet fresh fragrance that reminded the children of the scent of their other world flowers, and it was, besides, deliciously soft and yet springy to walk upon.

Waldo and Rollo came running back to meet the little girls, for Silva had quickly followed Maia.

'Isn't this a nice place?' said Rollo, jumping up and down as he spoke. 'We might run races here all the afternoon.'

'Yes; but we must hasten on,' said Silva. 'They're expecting us, you know. But we can run races all the same, for we've a good way along here to go. You and Waldo start first, and then Maia and I.'

So they did, and never was there a race pleasanter to run. They felt as if they had wings on their feet, they went so fast and were so untired. The moss gallery resounded with their laughter and merry cries, though their footfalls made no sound on the floor.

'What was the pattering we heard after Waldo knocked?' asked Maia suddenly.

'It was the squirrels overhead. They all have to run together to pull open the door,' said Silva. 'The rope goes up to their hall. But you will see it all for yourself now. This is the end of the gallery.'

'This' was a circular room, moss-lined like the passage, with a wide round hole in the roof, from which, as the children stood waiting, descended a basket, fitted with moss cushions, and big enough to hold all of them at once. In they got, and immediately the basket rose up again and stopped at what, in a proper house, one would call the next floor. And even before it stopped a whole mass of brown heads were to be seen eagerly watching for it, and numbers of little brown paws were extended to help the visitors to step out.

'Good-day, good-day,' squeaked a multitude of shrill voices; 'welcome to Squirrel-Land. We have been watching for you ever so long, since the pigeon brought the news. And the supper is all ready. The acorn cakes smelling so good and the chestnut pasties done to a turn.'

'Thank you, thank you, Mrs. Bushy!' said Silva. 'I am sure they will be excellent. But first, I must introduce our friends and you to each other. Maia and Rollo, this is Mrs. Bushy,' and as she said so the fattest and fussiest of the squirrels made a duck with its head and a flourish with its tail, which were meant for the most graceful of curtsies. 'Mr. Bushy —' she stopped and looked round.

'Alas! my dear husband is very lame with his gout to-day,' said Mrs. Bushy. 'He took too much exercise yesterday. I'm sure if he went once to the top of the tree he went twenty times–he is *so* active, you know; so he's resting in the supper-room; but you'll see him presently. And here are my dear children, Miss Silva. Stand forward, my dears, you have nothing to be ashamed of. *Do* look at their tails–though I say it that shouldn't, *did* you ever see such tails?' and Mrs. Bushy's bright eyes sparkled with maternal pride. 'There they are, all nine of them: Nibble, Scramble, Bunchy, Friskit, and Whiff, my dear boys; and Clamberina, Fluffy, Tossie, and sweet little Curletta, my no less beloved daughters.'

Whereupon each one of the nine, who had collected in a row, made the same duck with its head and flourish with its tail as Mrs. Bushy, though, of course, with somewhat less perfection of style and finish than their dear mamma.

'Such manners, such sweet manners!' she murmured confidentially to Silva and Maia.

Maia was by this time nearly choking with laughter —'Though I say it that shouldn't say it, I am sure you young ladies must be pleased with their sweet manners.'

'Very pleased, dear Mrs. Bushy,' said Silva; 'I'm sure they've learned to duck their heads and wave their tails beautifully.'

'Beautifully,' said Maia, at which Mrs. Bushy looked much gratified.

'And shall we proceed to supper, then?' she said. 'I am sure you must be hungry.'

'Yes, I think we are,' said Waldo; 'and I know your chestnut cakes are very good, Mrs. Bushy.'

Rollo and Maia looked at each other. *Chestnuts* were very nice, but what would chestnut cakes be like? Besides, it wasn't the season for chestnuts; they must be very old and stale.

'How can you have chestnuts now?' asked Maia. Mrs. Bushy looked at her patronisingly.

'Ah, to be sure,' she said, 'the young lady does not know all about our magic preserving cupboards, and all the newest improvements. To be sure, it is her first visit to Squirrel-Land,' she added encouragingly; 'we can make allowance. Now, lead the way, my dears, lead the way,' she said to her nine treasures, who thereupon set off with a rush, jumping and frisking and scuttering along, till Maia could hardly help bursting out laughing again, while she and Silva and Rollo and Waldo followed them into the supper-room, where, at the end of a long narrow table, covered with all sorts of queer-looking dishes, decorated with fern leaves, Papa Bushy, in a moss arm-chair, his tail comfortably waving over him like an umbrella, was already installed.

'I beg your pardon, my dear young friends,' he began, in a rather deeper, though still squeaky voice, 'for receiving you like this. Mrs. Bushy will have made my apologies. This unfortunate attack of gout! I am, I fear, too actively inclined, and have knocked myself up!'

'Ah, yes,' said Mrs. Bushy, shaking her head; 'I'm sure if Mr. Bushy goes once a day to the top of the tree, he goes twenty times.'

'But what does he go for if it makes him ill?' exclaimed Maia.

Mrs. Bushy looked at her and gasped, Mr. Bushy shut his eyes and waved his paws about as if to say, 'We must excuse her, she knows no better,' and all the young Bushys ducked their heads and squeaked faintly, —evidently Maia had said something very startling. At last, when she had to some extent recovered her self-control, Mrs. Bushy said faintly, looking round her for sympathy:

'Poor child! Such deplorable ignorance; but we must excuse it. Imagine her not knowing–imagine *any* one not knowing what would happen if Mr. Bushy did not go to the top of the tree!'

'What *would* happen?' said Maia, not sure if she felt snubbed or not, but not inclined to give in all at once.

'My poor child,' said Mrs. Bushy, in the most solemn tone her squeaky voice was capable of, '*the world would stop!*'

Maia stared at her, but what she was going to say I cannot tell you, for Silva managed to give her a little pinch, as a sign that she had better make no more remarks, and Mrs. Bushy, feeling that she had done her duty, requested everybody to take their places at table. The dishes placed before them were so comical-looking that Rollo and Maia did not know what to reply when asked what they would have.

'An apple, if you please!' said Maia, catching sight at last of something she knew the name of. But when Mrs. Bushy pressed her to try a chestnut cake she did not like to refuse, and seeing that Waldo and Silva were careful to eat like the squirrels, holding up both hands together like paws to their mouths, she and Rollo did the same, which evidently gave the Bushy family a better opinion of the way in which they had been brought up. The chestnut cakes were rather nice, but poor Rollo, having ventured on some fried acorns which smelt good, could not help pulling a very wry face. Supper, however, was soon over, and then Waldo and Silva asked leave very politely to go 'up the tree,' which in squirrel language was much the same as if they had asked to go out to the garden, and Mrs. Bushy, with many excuses for not accompanying them on account of her household cares, and Mr. Bushy, pleading his gout, told her nine darlings to escort the visitors upstairs.

Now began the real fun of the afternoon. A short flight of steps, like a little ladder, led them to the outside of the tree. The nine Bushys scampered and rushed along, squeaking and chattering with the greatest good-nature, followed more slowly by the four children. For a moment or two, when Rollo and Maia found themselves standing on a branch very near the top of the tree, though, strange to say, they found it wide enough to hold them quite comfortably, they felt rather giddy and frightened.

'How dreadfully high up we seem!' said Maia. 'Rollo, I'm *sure* we must have grown smaller. The trees never looked so big as this before. It makes me giddy to look either up or down.'

'You'll get used to it in a minute,' said Waldo. 'Silva and I don't mind it the least now. Look at the Bushys, Maia, isn't it fun to see them?'

And Maia forgot her fears in watching the nine young squirrels. Had Mrs. Bushy been with them, her maternal vanity would have been gratified by the admiration their exploits drew forth. It really was the funniest and prettiest sight in the world to see them at their gambols. No dancers on the tight-rope were ever half so clever. They swung themselves up by the branches to the very top of the tree, and then in an instant-flash! —there they were ever so far below where the children were standing. And in another instant, like a brown streak, up they were again, darting hither, there, and everywhere, so that one felt as if the whole tree were alive. When they had a little worked off their spirits they squeaked to the children to join them; Waldo and Silva did so at once, for they were used to these eccentric gymnastics, and to Rollo and Maia they looked nearly as clever as the squirrels themselves, as, holding on by their companions' paws and tails, they jumped and clambered and slid up and down. So in a little while the new-comers too took courage and found the performances, like many other things, not half so hard as they looked. And oh, how they all laughed and screamed, and how the squirrels squeaked with enjoyment! I don't think ever children before had such fun. Fancy the pleasure of swaying in a branch ever so far overhead quite safe, for there were the nine in a circle ready to catch you if you slipped, and then hand in hand, or rather hand in paw, dancing round the trunk by hopping two and two from branch to branch, nine squirrels and four children —a merry baker's dozen. Then the sliding down the tree, like a climber on a May-pole, was great fun too, for the Bushys had a way of twisting themselves round it so as to avoid the sticking-out branches that was really very clever. So that when suddenly, in the middle of it all, a little silvery tinkling bell was heard to ring, and they all stood still looking at each other, Rollo and Maia felt quite vexed at the interruption.

I don't think ever children before had such fun.

'Go on,' said Maia, 'what are you all stopping for?'

'The summons,' said Waldo and Silva together. 'We must go. Good-night, all of you,' to the squirrels. Had their mother been there, I fancy they would have addressed Clamberina and her brothers and sisters more ceremoniously. 'Good-bye, and thank you for all the fun.'

'Good-bye, and thank you,' said Rollo and Maia, rather at a loss as to whether they should offer to shake paws, or if that was not squirrel fashion. But before they had time to consider, 'Quick,' said a voice behind them, which they were not slow to recognise, 'slide down the tree,' and down they slid, all four, though, giving one glance upwards, they caught sight of the nine squirrels all seated in a row on a branch, each with their pocket-handkerchief at their eyes, weeping copiously.

'Poor things,' said Maia, 'how tender-hearted they are!'

'They always do that when we come away,' said Waldo; 'it's part of their manners. But they are very good-natured.'

'And where's godmother,' said Maia, when they found themselves on terra-firma again. 'Wasn't it her voice that spoke to us up on the tree, and told us to come down?'

'Yes,' said Silva; 'but she called up through a speaking-trumpet. I don't know where she is herself. She may be a good way off. But that doesn't matter. We can tell what to do. Lay your ear to the ground, Waldo.'

Waldo did so.

'Are they coming,' asked Silva.

'Yes,' said Waldo, getting up; 'they'll be here directly;' and almost before he had left off speaking the pretty sound of tinkling bells was heard approaching, nearer and nearer every second, till the children, to their delight, caught sight of the little carriage and the tiny piebald ponies, which came dancing up to them all of themselves, and stood waiting for them to get in.

'But where's godmother?' exclaimed Maia; 'how can we get home without her?'

'All right,' said Waldo; 'she often lends Silva and me her ponies. I can drive you home quite safely, you'll see. Get in, Maia and Silva behind-Rollo and I will go in front.'

And off they set. It was not quite such a harum-scarum drive as it had been coming. Waldo did not take any flying leaps-indeed, I think nobody but godmother herself could have managed that! but it was very delightful all the same.

'Oh, Silva,' exclaimed Maia, 'I do so wish we need not go back to the white castle and Lady Venelda and our lessons! I do so wish we might live in the cottage with you and Waldo, *always*.'

Silva looked a little sorry when Maia spoke thus.

'Don't say that, Maia,' she said. 'Godmother wouldn't like it. We want to make you happy while you're here-not to make you impatient. If you and Rollo were always at the cottage, you wouldn't like it half so much as you do now, coming sometimes. You would soon get tired of it, unless you worked hard like Waldo and me.'

'Do you work hard?' said Maia, with some surprise.

'Yes, of course we do. You only see us at our play-time. Waldo goes off to the forester's at the other side of the wood every morning at six, and I take him his dinner every day, and then I stay there and work in the dairy till we come home together in the evening.'

'But you sometimes have holidays,' said Maia.

'Yes, of course we do,' said Silva, smiling. 'Godmother sees to that.'

'How?' asked Maia. 'Does she know the forester and his wife? Does she go and ask them to give you a holiday?'

'Not exactly,' said Silva, smiling. 'I can't tell you how she does it. She has her own ways for doing everything. How does she get you *your* holidays?'

'Does *she* get us them?' said Maia, astonished. 'Why, Lady Venelda never speaks of her. Do you think she knows her?'

'I can't tell you,' said Silva, again smiling in the same rather strange way as before, and some-how when she smiled like that she reminded Maia of godmother herself; 'but she does know *somebody* at the white castle, and somebody there knows her.'

'The old doctor!' exclaimed Maia, clapping her hands. 'I'm *sure* you mean the old doctor. Ah! that's how it is, is it? Godmother sends to the old doctor or writes to him, or-or —I don't know what-and then he finds out we need a holiday, and-oh, he manages it somehow, I suppose!'

'Yes,' said Silva; 'but as long as you get your holiday it's all right. When godmother tells us of anything we're to do, or that she has settled for us, we're quite pleased without asking her all the little bits about it.'

'I see,' said Maia; 'but then, Silva, you're different from me.'

'Of course I am,' said Silva; 'but it wouldn't be at all nice if everybody was the same. That's one of the things godmother always says.'

'Yes, like what she says about how stupid it would be if we knew everything, and if there was nothing more to puzzle and wonder about. It *is* nice to wonder and puzzle sometimes, but not always. Just now I don't mind about anything except about the fun of going so fast, with those dear little ponies' bells tinkling all the way. I shall be so sorry to get to the cottage, for we shan't have time to go in, Silva. We shall have to hurry home not to be too late for supper.'

Just as she spoke Waldo pulled up sharply.

'What's the matter?' called out Maia. She had been talking so much to Silva that she had not noticed the way they were going. Now she looked about her, and it seemed to her that she recognised the look of the trees, which were much less close and thick than in the middle of the forest. But before she had time to think more about it a voice close at hand made both her and Rollo start.

'Well, young people,' it said, 'you have had, I hope, a pleasant day? You, too, Waldo and Silva? It is some time since I have seen you, my children.'

It was, of course, the voice of the doctor. All the four jumped out of the little carriage and ran forward to their old friend, for to Rollo's and Maia's surprise, the two forest children seemed to know him quite as well as they did themselves.

He seemed delighted to see them all, and his kind old face shone with pleasure as he patted the curly heads of the boys and Maia, and stroked gently Silva's pretty, smooth hair.

'But you must go home,' he said to Waldo and Silva. 'Good-night, my children;' and quickly bidding their little friends farewell, the brother and sister sprang up again into the tiny carriage, and in another moment the more and more faintly-tinkling bells were all left of them, as Rollo and Maia stood a little sadly, gazing in the direction in which they had disappeared.

'And you have been happy?' said the old doctor.

'*Very* happy,' both replied together. 'We have had such fun.' But before they had time to tell their old friend anything more he interrupted them.

'You, too, must hurry home,' he said. 'You see where you are? Up the path to the right and you will come out at the usual place just behind the castle wall at the back.'

Rollo and Maia hastened to obey him.

'How queer he is!' said Maia. 'He doesn't seem to care to hear what we've been doing-he never asks anything but if we've been happy.'

'Well, what does it matter?' said Rollo. 'I like only to talk to ourselves of the queer things we see when we're with Waldo and Silva. I wonder what they will show us or where they will take us the next time?'

'So do I,' said Maia.

'Waldo said something about the eagles that live up in the high rocks at the edge of the forest,' said Rollo. 'He did not exactly say so, but he spoke as if he had been there. Wouldn't you like to see an eagles' nest, Maia?'

'I should think so, indeed!' replied Maia eagerly. 'But I don't think that's what they call it, Rollo; there's another name.'

'Yes, I think there is, but I can't remember it,' he answered. 'But never mind, Maia, here we are at the gate. We must run in and get ready for supper.'

CHAPTER IX
A COMMITTEE OF BIRDS.

'Then a sound is heard,
A sudden rushing sound of many wings.'

Nothing was asked of the children as to where or how they had spent their day. Lady Venelda looked at them kindly as they took their places at the supper-table, and she kissed them when they said good-night as if she were quite pleased with them. They were not sorry to go to bed; for however delightful squirrel gymnastics are, they are somewhat fatiguing, especially to those who are not accustomed to them, and I can assure you that Rollo and Maia slept soundly that night; thanks to which, no doubt, they woke next morning as fresh as larks.

Their lessons were all done to the satisfaction of their teachers, so that in the afternoon, when, as they were setting off with Nanni for their usual walk, they met the old doctor on the terrace, he nodded at them good-humouredly.

'That's right,' he said; 'holidays do you no harm, I see.'

'And we may have another before very long, then, mayn't we?' said Maia, whose little tongue was always the readiest.

'All in good time,' said the old man, and as they had found his memory so good hitherto, the children felt that they might trust him for the future.

They did not go in the direction of the cottage to-day. Though they had not exactly been told so, they had come to understand that when godmother wanted them, or had arranged some pleasure for them and her forest children, she would find some means of letting them know, and the sort of desire to please and obey her which they felt seemed even stronger than if her wishes had been put down in plain rules. And when Nanni was with them they now took care not to speak of the cottage or their friends there, for she could not have understood about them, and she would only have been troubled and frightened. But yet the thought of Waldo and Silva and godmother and the cottage, and all the pleasure and fun they had had, seemed never quite away. It hovered about them like the impression of a happy dream, which seems to make the whole day brighter, though we can scarcely tell how.

The spring was now coming on fast; and what *can* be more delightful than spring-time in the woods? With the increasing warmth and sunshine the scent of the pines seemed to waft out into the air, the primroses and violets opened their eyes, and the birds overhead twittered and trilled in their perfect happiness.

'How can any one be so cruel as to shoot them?' said Maia one afternoon about a week after the visit to the squirrels.

'I don't think any one would shoot these tiny birds,' said Rollo.

'I am afraid they do in some countries,' said Maia. 'Not here; I don't think godmother would let them. I think nobody can do anything in these woods against her wishes,' she went on in a lower tone, glancing in Nanni's direction. But that young woman was knitting away calmly, with an expression of complete content on her rosy face.

'Rollo,' Maia continued, 'come close to me. I want to speak in a whisper;' and Rollo, who, like his sister, was stretched at full length on the ground, thickly carpeted with the tiny dry-brown spikes which had fallen from the fir-trees during the winter, edged himself along by his elbows without getting up, till he was near enough to hear Maia's lowest murmur.

'Lazy boy,' she said, laughing. 'Is it too much trouble to move?'

'It's too much trouble to stand up any way,' replied Rollo. 'What is it you want to say, Maia? I do think there's something in these woods that puts one to sleep, as Nanni says.'

'So do I,' said Maia, and her voice had a half sleepy sound as she spoke. 'I don't quite know what I wanted to say, Rollo. It was only something about *them*, you know.'

'You needn't be the least afraid-Nanni can't hear,' said Rollo, without moving.

'Well, I only wanted to talk a little about them. Just to wonder, you know, if they won't soon be sending for us-making some new treat. It seems such a long time since we saw them.'

'Only a week,' said Rollo, sleepily.

'Well, a week's a good while,' pursued Maia; 'and I'm sure we've done our lessons *very* well all this time, and nobody's had to scold us for anything. *Rollo* — —'

'Oh, I do wish you'd let me take a little sleep,' said poor Rollo.

'Oh, very well, then! I won't talk if you want to go to sleep,' said Maia, in a slightly offended tone; 'though I must say I think it is very stupid of you when we've been shut up at our lessons all the morning, and we have only an hour to stay out, to want to spend it all in sleeping.'

But she said no more, for by this time Rollo was quite asleep, and the click-click of Nanni's knitting-needles grew fainter and fainter, till Maia, looking round to see why she was stopping, discovered that Nanni too had given in to the influence of the woods. She was asleep, and doubtless dreaming pleasantly, for there was a broad smile on her good-natured face.

'Stupid things!' thought Maia to herself. And then she began wondering what amusement she could find till it was time to go home again. 'For *I'm* not sleepy,' she said; 'it is only the twinkling way the sunshine comes through the trees that makes my eyes feel rather dazzled. I may as well shut them a little, and as I have no one to talk to I will try to say over my French poetry, so that I shall know it *quite* well for Mademoiselle Delphine to-morrow morning.'

The French poetry was long and dull. The complaint of a shepherdess for the loss of her sheep was the name of it, and Maia had not found it easy to learn, for, like many things it was then the custom to teach children, it was neither interesting nor instructive. But if it did her good in no other way, it was a lesson of patience, and Maia had worked hard at it. She now began to say it over to herself from the beginning in a low monotonous voice, her eyes closed as she half lay, half sat, leaning her head on the trunk of one of the great trees. It seemed to her that her poetry went wonderfully well. Never before had it sounded to her so musical. She really felt quite a pleasure in softly murmuring the lines, and quite unconsciously they seemed to set themselves to an air she had often been sung to sleep to by her nurse when a very little girl, till to her surprise Maia found herself singing in a low but exquisitely sweet voice.

'I *never* knew I could sing so beautifully,' she thought to herself; 'I must tell Rollo about it.' But she did not feel inclined to wake him up to listen to it. She had indeed forgotten all about him being asleep at her side-she had forgotten everything but the beauty of her song and the pleasure of her newly-discovered talent. And on and on she sang, like the bewitched Princess, though what she was singing about she could not by this time have told, till all of a sudden she became aware that she was not singing alone-or, at least, not without an accompaniment. For all through her singing, sometimes rising above it, sometimes gently sinking below, was a sweet trilling warble, purer and clearer than the sound of a running brook, softer and mellower than the music of any instrument Maia had ever heard.

'What can it be?' thought Maia. She half determined to open her eyes to look, but she refrained from a vague fear that if she did so it might perhaps scare the music away. But unconsciously she had stopped singing, and just then a new sound as of innumerable wings close to her made her forget all in her curiosity to see what it was. She opened her eyes in time to see fluttering downwards an immense flock of birds-birds of every shape and colour, though none of them were very big, the largest being about the size of a parrot. There lay Rollo, fast asleep, in the midst of the crowd of feathered creatures, and something-an instinct she could not explain-made Maia quickly shut her eyes again. She was not afraid, but she felt sure the birds would not have come so near had they not thought her asleep too. So she remained perfectly still, leaning her head against the trunk of the tree and covering her face with her hand, so that she could peep out between the fingers while yet seeming to be asleep.

The flutter gradually ceased, and the great flock of birds settled softly on the ground. Then began a clear chirping which, to Maia's delight, as she listened with all her ears, gradually seemed to shape itself into words which she could understand.

'Do you think they liked our music?' piped a bird, or several birds together-it was impossible to say which.

'I think so,' answered some other; 'he' —and Maia understood that they were speaking of Rollo —'has heard it but dimly-he is farther away. But she was nearer us and will not forget it.'

'They seem good children,' said in a more squeaky tone a black and white bird, hopping forward a little by himself. He appeared to Maia to be some kind of crow or raven, but she disliked his rather patronising tone.

'Good children,' she said to herself. 'What business has an old crow to talk of us as good children!'

'Ah, yes!' replied a little brown bird which had established itself on a twig just above Rollo's head. 'If they had not been so, you may be sure she would have had nothing to do with them, instead of making them as happy as she can, and giving orders all through the forest that they are to be entertained. I hear they amused themselves very well at the squirrels' the other day.'

'Ah, indeed! A party?'

'Oh, no-just a simple gambolade. Had it been a party, of course our services would have been retained for the music.'

'Naturally,' replied the little brown bird. 'Of course no musical entertainment would be complete without you, Mr. Crow.'

The old black bird giggled. He seemed quite flattered, and was evidently on the point of replying to his small brown friend by some amiable speech, when a soft cooing voice interrupted him. It was that of a wood-pigeon, who, with two or three companions, came hopping up to them.

'What are we to do?' she said. 'Shall we warble a slumber-song for them? They are sleeping still.'

The old crow glanced at the children.

'I fancy they have had enough music for to-day,' he said. 'I think we should consult together seriously about what we can do for their entertainment. It won't do to let the squirrels be the only ones to show them attention. Besides, children who come to our woods and amuse themselves without ever robbing a nest, catching a butterfly, or causing the slightest alarm to even a hare-such children deserve to be rewarded.'

'What can we do for them?' chirruped a brisk little robin. 'We have given them a concert, which has had the effect' —and he made a patronising little bow in the direction of Rollo and Maia —'the effect-of sending them to sleep.'

'I beg your pardon,' said a sparrow pertly. 'They were asleep before our serenade began. It was intended to lull their slumbers. That was her desire.'

'Doubtless,' said the crow snappishly. 'Mr. Sparrow is always the best informed as to matters in the highest quarters. And, of course-considering his world-wide fame as a songster — —'

'No sparring-no satirical remarks, gentlemen,' put in a bird who had not yet spoken. It was a blackbird, and all listened to him with respect. 'We should give example of nothing but peace and unity to these unfeathered visitors of ours, otherwise they might carry away a most mistaken idea of our habits and principles and of the happiness in which we live.'

'Certainly-certainly,' agreed the crow. 'It was but a little amiable repartee, Mr. Blackbird. My young friend Sparrow has not quite thrown off the-the slight-sharpness of tone acquired, almost unconsciously, by a long residence in cities.'

'And you, my respected friend,' observed the sparrow, 'are naturally-but we can all make allowance for each other-not altogether indisposed to croak. But these are trifling matters in no way interfering with the genuine brotherliness and good feeling in which we all live together in this favoured land.'

A gentle but general buzz, or twitter rather, of applause greeted this speech.

'And now to business,' said the robin. 'What are we to arrange for the amusement of our young friends?'

'A remark reached my ears —I may explain, in passing, that some members of my family have a little nest just under the eaves of the castle, and-and —I now and then hear snatches of conversation-not, of course, that we are given to *eavesdropping* —of course, none of my family could be suspected of such a thing-but, as I was saying, a remark reached my ears that our young friends would like to visit what, in human language, would be called our king's palace-that is to say, the eyrie of the great eagle at the summit of the forest,' said a swallow, posing his awkward body ungracefully on one leg and looking round for approval.

'Nothing easier,' replied the robin. 'We are much obliged to you for the suggestion, Mr. Swallow. If it meets with approval in the highest quarters, I vote that we should carry it out.'

Another twitter of approval greeted this speech.

'And when shall the visit take place?' asked the wood-pigeon softly, 'and how shall it be accomplished?'

'As to *when*, that is not for us to decide,' said the robin. 'As to *how*, I should certainly think a voyage through the air would be far the greatest novelty and amusement. And this, by laying our wings all together, we can easily arrange. The first thing we have to do is to submit the idea for approval, and then we can all meet together again and fix the details. But now I think we should be on the wing to regain our nests. Besides, our young friends will be awaking soon. It would not do for them to see us here assembled in such numbers. It might alarm them.'

'That is true,' said the crow. 'Their education in some respects has been neglected. They have not enjoyed the unusual advantages of Waldo and Silva. But still-they are very good children, in their way.'

This last speech made Maia so angry that, forgetting all pretence of being asleep, she started up to give the old crow a bit of her mind.

'You impertinent old croaker,' she began to say, but to her amazement there was neither crow nor bird of any kind to be seen! Maia rubbed her eyes-was she, or had she been dreaming? No, it was impossible. But yet, how had all the birds got away so quickly, without the least flutter or bustle, and in less than half a second? She turned to Rollo and gave him a shake.

'Rollo,' she said, 'do wake up, you lazy boy. Where have they all gone to?'

CHAPTER X
A SAIL IN THE AIR.

'Bright are the regions of the air,
And among the winds and beams

It were delight to wander there.'

SHELLEY.

'What are you talking about?' said Rollo, sitting up, and in his turn rubbing his eyes. 'Where have "who" gone to?'

'The birds, of course,' replied Maia. 'You can't be so stupid, Rollo, as not to have seen them.'

'I've been asleep,' said the poor boy, looking rather ashamed of himself. 'What birds were they? Did you see them? I have a queer sort of feeling,' and he hesitated, looking at Maia as if she could explain it, 'as if I had dreamt something about them-as if I heard some sort of music through my sleep. What did *you* see, Maia? do tell me.'

Maia described it all to him, and he listened with the greatest interest. But at the end he made an observation which roused her indignation.

'I believe you were dreaming too,' he said. 'Nobody ever heard of birds speaking like that.'

'And yet you say you heard something of it through your sleep? Is it likely we both dreamt the same thing all of ourselves?'

'But I didn't dream that birds were talking,' objected Rollo. 'They can't talk.'

Maia glanced at him with supreme contempt.

'Can squirrels talk?' she said. 'Would anybody believe all the things we have seen and done since we have been in this Christmas-tree land? Think of our drives in godmother's carriage; think of our finding our way through a tree's trunk; think of godmother herself, with her wonderful ways and her beautiful dress, and yet that she can look like a poor old woman! Would anybody believe all that, do you think? And we know it's all true; and yet you can't believe birds can talk! Oh, you are too stupid.'

Rollo smiled; he did not seem vexed.

'I don't see that all that prevents it being possible that you were dreaming all the same,' he said. 'But dreams are true sometimes.'

'Are they?' said Maia, looking puzzled in her turn. 'Well, what was the use of going on so about birds never talking, then? Never mind, now; just wait and see if what I've told you doesn't come true. *I* shall go, Rollo; if the birds come to fetch us to go to see the eagle, *I* shall go.'

'So shall I,' said Rollo coolly. 'I never had the slightest intention of not going. But we must go home now, Maia; it's getting late, and you know we were not to stay long to-day.'

'Where's Nanni?' said Maia.

'Perhaps the birds have flown off with her,' said Rollo mischievously. But for a moment or two neither he nor Maia could help feeling a little uneasy, for no Nanni was to be seen! They called her and shouted to her, and at last a sort of grunt came in reply, which guided them to where, quite hidden by a little nest of brushwood, Nanni lay at full length, blinking her eyes as if she had not the slightest idea where she was.

As soon as she saw them, up she jumped.

'Oh, I am so ashamed,' she cried. 'What could have come over me to fall asleep like that, just when I thought I should have got such a great piece of Master Rollo's stockings done! And you have been looking for me, lazy girl that I am! But I can assure you, Miss Maia, when I first sat down I was not here —I was sitting over there,' and she pointed to another tree-stump a little way off, 'not asleep at all, and knitting so fast. There are fairies in the wood, Miss Maia,' she added in a lower voice. 'I've thought it many a time, and I'm more sure than ever of it now. I don't think we should come into the woods at all, I really don't.'

'We shouldn't have anywhere to walk in, then,' said Rollo. 'I don't see why you should be afraid of fairies, Nanni, even supposing there are any. They've never done us any harm. Now, have they?'

But though she could not say they had, Nanni did not look happy. She was one of those people that did not like anything she did not understand. Maia gave Rollo's sleeve a little pull as a sign to him that he had better not say any more, and then they set off quickly walking back to the castle.

For some days things went on as usual, though every morning when she got up and every evening when she went to bed Maia wondered if the summons would not come soon. She went all round the castle, peeping up into the eaves to see if she could find the swallows' nest; but she did not succeed, and it was no wonder, for the solitary nest was hidden away in a corner where even Maia's sharp eyes could not penetrate, and the swallows flew out and in through a hole in the parapet round the roof which no one suspected.

'I know there *are* swallows here,' she said to Rollo, 'for I've seen them. But I can't fancy where they live.'

'Nanni would say they were fairies,' said Rollo, smiling. He was more patient than his sister, and he was quite sure that godmother would not forget them. And by degrees Maia began to follow his example, especially after Rollo happened to remark one day that he had noticed that it was always when they had been working the most steadily at their lessons, and thinking the least of holidays and treats that the holidays and treats came. This counsel Maia took to heart, and worked so well for some days that Mademoiselle Delphine and the old chaplain had none but excellent reports to give of both children, and Lady Venelda smiled on them so graciously that they felt sure her next letter to their father would be a most satisfactory one.

One evening-it was the evening of a most lovely spring day-when Rollo and Maia had said good-night in the usual ceremonious way to Lady Venelda, they were coming slowly along the great corridor, white like the rest of the castle, which led to their own rooms, when a sound at one of the windows they were passing made them stop.

'What was that?' said Maia. 'It sounded like a great flutter of wings.'

Rollo glanced out of the window. It was nearly dark, but his eyes were quick.

'It was wings,' he said. 'Quite a flight of birds have just flown off from under the roof.'

'Ah,' said Maia, nodding her head mysteriously, 'I thought so. Well, Rollo, *I* don't intend to go to sleep to-night, whether you do or not.'

Rollo shook his head.

'I shall wake if there's anything to wake for,' he said. 'I'm much more sure of doing that than you can be of keeping awake.'

'Why, I couldn't *go* to sleep if I thought there was going to be anything to wake for,' said Maia.

Before long they were both in bed. Rollo laid his head on the pillow without troubling himself about keeping awake or going to sleep. Maia, on the contrary, kept her eyes as wide open as she could. It was a moonlight night; the objects in the room stood out in sharp black shadow against the bright radiance, seeming to take queer fantastic forms which made her every minute start up, feeling sure that she saw some one or something beside her bedside. And every time that she found it a mistake she felt freshly disappointed. At last, quite tired with expecting she knew not what, she turned her face to the wall and shut her eyes.

'Stupid things that they all are!' she said to herself. 'Godmother, and the birds, and Waldo, and Silva, and the old doctor, and everybody. They've no business to promise us treats, and then never do anything about them. I shan't think any more about it, that I won't. I believe it's all a pretence.'

Which you will, I am sure, agree with me in thinking not very reasonable on Maia's part!

She fell asleep at last, and, as might have been expected, much more soundly than usual. When she woke, it was from a deep, dreamless slumber, but with the feeling that for some time some one had been calling her, and that she had been slow of rousing herself.

'What is it?' she called out, sitting up in bed, and trying to wink the sleep out of her eyes. 'Who is there?'

'Maia!' a voice replied. A voice that seemed to come from a great distance, and yet to reach her as clearly as any sound she had ever heard in her life. 'Maia, are you ready?'

Up sprang Maia.

'Godmother, is it you calling me?' she said. 'Oh, yes, it must be you! I'll be ready in a moment, godmother. If I could but find my shoes and stockings! Oh, dear! oh, dear! and I meant to keep awake all night. I've been expecting you such a long time.'

'I know,' said the voice, quite close beside her this time; 'you have been expecting me too much,' and, glancing round, Maia saw in the moonlight-right *in* the moonlight, looking indeed almost as if the bright rays came from her —a shadowy silvery figure, quite different from god-mother as she had hitherto known her, but which, nevertheless, she knew in a moment could be no one else. Maia flung her arms round her and kissed her.

'Yes,' she said, 'now I'm *quite* sure it's you and not a dream. No dream has cheeks so soft as yours, godmother, and no one else kisses like you. Your kisses are just like violets. But what am I to do? Must I get dressed at once?'

Godmother passed her hands softly round the child. She seemed to stroke her.

'You are dressed,' she said. 'The clothes you wear generally would be too heavy, so I brought some with me. You do not need shoes and stockings.'

But Maia was looking at herself with too much surprise almost to hear what she said. 'Dressed,' yes, indeed! She was dressed as never before in her life, and though she turned herself about, and stroked herself like a little bird proud of its plumage, she could not find out of what her dress was made, nor what exactly was its colour. Was it velvet, or satin, or plush? Was it green or blue?

'I know,' she cried at last joyously; 'it's the same stuff your red dress is made of, godmother! Oh, how nice, and soft, and warm, and light all together it is! I feel as if I could jump up to the sky.'

'And not be seen when you got there,' said godmother. 'The colour of your dress *is* sky colour, Maia. But when you have finished admiring yourself we must go-the others have been ready ever so long. They had not been expecting me *too* much, like you, and so they were ready all the quicker.'

'Do you mean Rollo?' said Maia. 'Rollo, and Silva, and Waldo?'

Godmother nodded her head.

'I'm ready now, any way,' said Maia.

'Give me your hand,' said godmother, and taking it she held it firm, and led Maia to the window. To the little girl's surprise it was wide open. Godmother, still holding her hand, softly whistled-once, twice, three times. Then stood quietly waiting.

A gentle, rustling, wafting sound became gradually audible. Maia remained perfectly still-holding her breath in her curiosity to see what was coming next. The sound grew nearer and louder, if one can use the word loud to so soft and delicate a murmur. Maia stretched out her head.

'Here they are,' said godmother, and as she spoke, a large object, looking something like a ship with two great sails swimming through the air instead of on the sea, came in sight, and, as if steered by an invisible hand, came slowly up to the window and there stopped.

'What is it?' cried Maia, not quite sure, in spite of godmother's firm clasp, whether she was not a little frightened, for even godmother herself looked strangely shadowy and unreal in the moonlight, and the great air-boat was like nothing Maia had ever seen or dreamt of. Suddenly she gave a joyful spring, for she caught sight of what took away all her fear. There in the centre of the huge sails, seated in a sort of car, and joyfully waving their hands to her, were Rollo, and Silva, and Waldo.

'Come, Maia,' they called out; 'the birds have come to fetch us, you see. There's a snug seat for you among the cushions. Come, quick.'

How was she to come, Maia was on the point of asking, when she felt godmother draw her quickly forward.

'Spring, my child, and don't be afraid,' she said, and Maia sprang almost without knowing it, for before she had time to ask or think anything about it, she found herself being kissed by Silva, and comfortably settled in her place by the boys.

'All right-we're off now,' Waldo called out, and at once, with a steady swing, the queer ship rose into the air.

'All right-we're off now,' Waldo called out, and at once, with a steady swing, the queer ship rose into the air.

'But godmother,' exclaimed Maia, 'where is she? Isn't she coming with us?'

'I am with you, my child,' answered godmother's clear, well-known voice. But where it came from Maia could not tell.

'Godmother is steering us,' said Silva softly, 'but we can't see her. She doesn't want us to see her. But she'll take care of us.'

'But where are we?' asked Maia bewildered. 'What is this queer ship or balloon that we are in? What makes it go?'

'Look closer, and you'll see,' said Silva. 'Look at the sails.'

And Maia looking, saw by the bright moonlight something stranger than any of the strange things she had yet seen in Christmas-tree land. The sails were made of an immense collection of birds all somehow or other holding together. Afterwards Silva explained to her that they were all clinging by their claws to a great frame, round which they were arranged in order according to their size, and all flapping their wings in perfect time, so as to have much the same effect in propelling the vessel through the air as the regular motion of several pairs of oars in rowing a boat over the sea. And gradually, as Maia watched and understood, a soft murmur reached her ears-it was the waft of the many pairs of wings as they all together clove the air.

'Oh, the dear, sweet birds!' she exclaimed. 'They have planned it all themselves, I am sure. Oh, Silva, isn't it lovely? Have you ever had a sail in the air like this before?'

'Not exactly like this,' said Silva.

'We've had *rides* in the air,' said Waldo mysteriously.

'*Have* you?' said Maia eagerly. 'Oh, do tell us about them!'

But Rollo laid his hand on her arm.

'Hush!' he said softly; 'the birds are going to sing,' and before Maia had time to ask him how he knew, the song began.

'Shut your eyes,' said Waldo; 'let's all shut our eyes. It sounds ever so much prettier.'

The others followed his advice. You can imagine nothing more delicious than the feeling of floating-for it felt more like quick floating than anything else-swiftly through the air, with the sweet warbling voices all keeping perfect time together, so that even the queer sounds which now and then broke through the others —a croak from the crow, who was quite satisfied that he alone conducted the bass voices, or a sudden screech from an owl, who had difficulty in subduing his tones-did not seem to mar the effect of the whole. The children did not speak; they did not feel as if they cared to do so. They held each others' hands, and Maia leant her head on Silva's shoulder in perfect content. It was like a beautiful dream.

Gradually the music ceased, and just as it did so godmother's well-known voice came clearly through the air. It seemed to come from above, and yet it sounded so near.

'Children,' she said, 'we are going higher. It will be colder for a while, for we must hasten, to be in good time for the dawn. Wrap yourselves up well!'

And as she spoke down dropped on their heads a great soft fleecy shawl or mantle. Softer and fleecier and lighter than any eider-down or lambs' wool that ever was seen or felt, and warmer too, for the children had but to give it the tiniest pull or pat in any direction and there it settled itself in the most comfortable way, creeping round them like the gentle hand of a mother covering up the little ones at night.

'It must be godmother who is tucking us up, though we can't see her,' said Rollo.

'Dear godmother,' said Maia, and a sort of little echo was murmured all round, even the birds seeming to join in it, of 'dear godmother.'

It did get colder, much colder; but the well-protected children, nestling in the cushions of their air-boat, did not feel it, except when inquisitive Maia poked up her sharp little nose, very quickly to withdraw it again.

'Oh, it *is* so freezy,' she said. 'My nose feels as if it would drop off. Do rub it for me, Silva.'

'I told you it would be cold,' said godmother's voice again. 'Stay where you are, Maia; indeed, I think I don't need to warn you now. A burnt child dreads the fire. I will tell you all when the time comes for you to peep out.'

Maia felt a very little ashamed of her restlessness, and for the rest of the journey she was perfectly quiet. Especially when in a few moments the birds began to sing again-still more softly and sweetly this time, so that it seemed a kind of cradle song. Whether the children slept or not I cannot tell. I don't think they could have told themselves; but in any case they were very still for a good long while after the serenade had ceased.

And then once more-clearer and more ringing than before-sounded godmother's voice.

'Children, look out! The dawn is breaking.'

And as the strange air-boat slowly relaxed its speed, floating downwards in the direction of some great cliffs almost exactly underneath where it was, the four children sat up, throwing off the fairy mantle which had so well protected them, and gazed with all their eyes, as well they might, at the wonderful beauty of the sight before them.

For they had sailed up to the eagles' eyrie in time to see the sun rise!

CHAPTER XI
THE EAGLES' EYRIE.

'Where, yonder, in the upper air
The solemn eagles watch the sun.'

Did you ever see the sun rise? I hope so; but still I am sure you never saw it from such a point as that whereon their winged conductors gently deposited the castle and the forest children that early summer morning.

'Jump out,' said the voice they had all learnt to obey, when the air-boat came to a stand-still a few feet above the rock. And the children, who as yet had noticed nothing of the ground above which they were hovering, for their eyes were fixed on the pink and azure and emerald and gold, spreading out like a fairy kaleidoscope on the sky before them, joined hands and sprang fearlessly on to they knew not what. And as they did so, with a murmuring warble of farewell, the birds flapped their wings, and the air-boat rose swiftly into the air and disappeared from view.

The four looked at each other.

'Has godmother sailed away in it? I thought she was going to stay with us,' exclaimed Maia in a disappointed tone.

'Oh, Maia,' said Silva, 'you don't yet understand godmother a bit. But we must not stand here. You know the way, Waldo?'

'Here,' where they were standing, was, as I said, a rock, ragged and bare, though lower down, its sides were clothed with short thymy grass. And stretching behind them the children saw a beautiful expanse of hilly ground, beautiful though treeless, for the heather and bracken and gorse that covered it looked soft and mellow in the distance, more especially with the lovely light and colour just now reflected from the sky.

But Waldo turned in the other direction. He walked a little way across the hard, bare rock, which he seemed to be attentively examining, till suddenly he stopped short, and tapped on the ground with a little stick he had in his hand.

'It must be about here,' he said. The other three children came close round him.

'Here,' exclaimed Silva, and she pointed to a small white cross cut in the stone at their feet.

Waldo knelt down, and pressed the spot exactly in the centre of the cross. Immediately a large slab of rock, forming a sort of door, but fitting so closely when shut that no one would have suspected its existence, opened inwards, disclosing a flight of steps. Waldo looked round.

'This is the short cut to the face of the cliff,' he said. 'Shall I go down first?'

'Yes, and I next,' said Rollo, eagerly springing forward.

Then followed Silva and Maia. The flight of steps was a short one. In a few moments they found themselves in a rocky passage, wide enough for them to walk along comfortably, one by one, and not dark, as light came in from little shafts cut at intervals in the roof. The passage twisted and turned about a good deal, but suddenly Waldo stopped, calling out:

'Here we are! Is not this worth coming to see?'

The passage had changed into a gallery, with the rock on one side only, on the other a railing, to protect those walking along it from a possible fall; for they were right on the face of an enormous cliff, far down at the bottom of which they could distinguish the tops of their old friends the firs. And far as the eye could reach stretched away into the distance, miles and miles and miles, here rising, there again sweeping downwards, the everlasting Christmas-trees!

The passage stopped suddenly. It ended in a sort of little shelf in the rock, and higher up in the wall, at the back of this shelf as it were, the children saw two large round holes cut in the rock: they were the windows of the eagles' eyrie.

Waldo went forward, and with his little stick tapped three times on the smooth, shining rock-wall. But the others, intently watching though they were, could not see how a door opened-whether it drew back inwards or rolled in sideways. All they saw was that just before them, where a moment before there had been the rock-surface, a great arched doorway now invited them to enter.

Waldo glanced round, though without speaking. The other three understood, and followed him through the doorway, which, in the same mysterious way in which it had opened, was now closed up behind them. But that it was so they hardly noticed, so delighted were they with what they saw before them. It was the prettiest room, or hall, you could imagine-the roof rising very high, and the light coming in through the two round windows of which I told you. And the whole-roof, walls, floor-was completely lined with what, at first sight, the children took for some most beautifully-embroidered kind of velvet. But velvet it was not. No embroidery ever showed the exquisite delicacy of tints, fading into each other like the softest tones of music, from the purest white through every silvery shade to the richest purple, or from deep glowing scarlet to pink paler than the first blush of the peach-blossom, while here and there rainbow wreaths shone out like stars on a glowing sky. It was these wreaths that told the secret.

'Why,' exclaimed Maia, 'it is all *feathers*!'

'Yes,' said Silva, 'I had forgotten. I never was here before, but godmother told me about it.'

'And where ——?' Maia was going on, but a sound interrupted her. It was that of a flutter of wings over their heads, and looking up the children perceived two enormous birds slowly flying downwards to where they stood, though whence they had come could not be seen.

They alighted and stood together-their great wings folded, while their piercing eyes surveyed their guests.

'We make you welcome,' they said at last, in a low soft tone which surprised the children, whose heads were full of the idea that eagles were fierce and their only voice a scream. 'We have been looking for your visit, of which our birds gave us notice. We have ordered a collation to be prepared for you, and we trust you will enjoy the view.'

Waldo, who seemed to be master of the ceremonies to-day, stepped forward a little in front of the others.

'We thank you,' he said quietly, making his best bow as he spoke.

The eagle queen raised her great wing-the left wing-and with it pointed to a spot among the feather hangings where, though they had not noticed it, the children now saw gleaming a silver knob.

'Up that stair leads to the balcony overhanging the cliff,' she said. 'There you will find our respected attendants, the falcon and the hawk, who have purveyed for your wants. And before you leave, the king and I hope to show you something of this part of our domains. *Au revoir!* —the sun awaits us to bid him good-morning.'

And with a slow, majestic movement the two strange birds spread their wings and rose up-wards, where, though the children's eyes followed them closely, they disappeared they knew not how or where.

Then Waldo turned the silver knob and opened a door, through which, as the eagle queen had said, they saw a staircase mounting straight upwards. It led out on to a balcony cut in the rock, but carefully carpeted with moss, and with rustic seats and a rustic table, on which were laid out four covers evidently intended for the four children. Two birds, large, but very much smaller than the eagles, stood at the side, each with a table-napkin over one wing, which so amused the children that it was with difficulty they returned the exceedingly dignified 'reverence' with which the hawk and the falcon greeted them. And they were rather glad when the two attendants spread their wings and flew over the edge of the balcony, evidently going to fetch the dishes.

'What will they give us to eat, I wonder?' said Maia. 'I hope it won't be pieces of poor little lambs, all raw, you know. That's what they always tell you eagles eat in the natural history books.'

'Not the eagles of *this* country,' said Silva. 'I am sure you never read about them in your books. *Our* eagles are not cruel and fierce; they would never eat little lambs.'

'But they must kill lots of little birds, whether they eat them or not,' said Maia, 'to get all those quantities and quantities of feathers.'

'Kill the little birds!' cried Silva and Waldo both at once. 'Kill their own birds! Maia, what are you thinking of? As if any creature that lives in Christmas-tree Land would kill any other! Why, the feathers are the birds' presents to the king and queen. They keep all that drop off and bring them once a year, and that's been done for years and years, till the whole of the nest is lined with them.'

'How nice!' replied Maia. 'I'm very glad the eagles are so kind. But they're not so *funny* as the squirrels. They look so very solemn.'

'They must be solemn,' said Waldo. 'They're not like the squirrels, who have nothing to do but jump about.'

'I beg your pardon,' said Rollo. 'Have you forgotten that the world would stop if Mr. Bushy didn't climb to the top of the tree?'

'And what would happen if the eagles left off watching the sun?' said Waldo.

'I don't know,' said Maia eagerly. 'Do tell us, Waldo.'

Waldo looked at her.

'I don't know either,' he said. 'Perhaps the sun would go to sleep, and then there would be a nice confusion.'

'You're laughing at me,' said Maia, in rather an offended tone. 'I don't see how I'm to be expected to know everything; if the squirrels and the eagles and all the creatures here are different from everywhere else, how could I tell?'

'Here's the collation!' exclaimed Rollo, and looking up, the others saw the falcon and the hawk flying back again, carrying between them a large basket, from which, when they had set it down beside the table, they cleverly managed, with beaks and claws, to take all sorts of mysterious things, which they arranged upon the table. There was no lamb, either raw or roasted, for all the repast consisted of fruits. Fruits of every kind the children had ever heard of, and a great many of which they did not even know the names, but which were more delicious than you, who have never tasted them, can imagine.

'You see the eagle king and queen have no need to kill poor little lambs,' said Silva. And Maia agreed with her that no one who could get such fruits to eat, need ever wish for any other food. While she was speaking, the same soft rustle which they had heard before sounded overhead, and again the two great majestic birds alighted beside them. The four children started to their feet.

'Thank you so much for the delicious fruit, eagle king and eagle queen,' said Maia, who was seldom backward at making speeches.

'We are glad you found it to your taste,' said the king. 'It has come from many a far-away land—lands you have perhaps scarcely even dreamt of, but which to us seem not so strange or distant.'

'Do you fly away so very far?' asked Maia, but the eagles only gleamed at her with their wonderful eyes, and shook their heads.

'It is not for us to tell what you could not understand,' said the king. 'They who can gaze undazzled on the sun must see many things.'

Maia drew back a little.

'They frighten me rather,' she whispered to the others. 'They are so solemn and mysterious.'

'But that needn't frighten you,' said Silva. 'Rollo isn't frightened.'

'Rollo's a boy,' replied Maia, as if that settled the matter.

Waldo now pointed out some steps in the rock leading up still higher.

'The eagles want us to go up there,' he said. 'We shall see right over the forest and ever so far.'

And so they did, for the steps led up a long way till they ended on another rock-shelf right on the face of the cliff. From here the great fir-forests looked but like dark patches far below, while away, away in the distance stretched on one side the great plain across which the children had journeyed on their first coming to the white castle; and on the other the distant forms of mountain ranges, gray-blue, shading fainter and fainter till the clouds themselves looked more real.

It was cold, very cold, up here on the edge of the great bare rocks. The beauty of the sunrise had sobered down into the chilly freshness of an early summer morning; the world seemed still asleep, and the children shivered a little.

'I don't think I should like to live always as high up as this,' said Maia. 'It's very lonely and very cold.'

'You would need to be dressed in feathers like the eagles if you did,' replied Silva; 'and if one had eyes like theirs, I dare say one would never feel lonely. One would see so much.'

'I wonder,' said Maia-and then she stopped.

'What were you going to say?' asked Rollo.

Maia's eyes looked far over the plain as if, like the eagles, they would pierce the distance.

'It was from there we came,' she said. 'I wonder if it will be from there that father will come to take us away. Do you think that the eagles will know when he is coming? do you think they will see him from very far off?'

Silva looked over the plain without speaking, and into her dark eyes there crept something that was not in Maia's blue ones.

'Maia,' exclaimed Rollo reproachfully, 'Silva is crying. She doesn't like you to talk of us going away.'

In an instant Maia's arms were round Silva's neck.

'Don't cry, Silva-you mustn't,' she said. 'When we go away you and Waldo shall come too-we will ask our father, won't we, Rollo?'

'And godmother?' said Silva, smiling again. 'What would she say? We are her children, Maia, and the children of the forest. We should not be fit to live as you do in the great world of men out away there. No; we can always love each other, and perhaps you and Rollo will come away out of the world sometimes to see us-but we must stay in our own country.'

'Never mind-don't talk about it just now,' said Maia. 'I wish I hadn't said anything about father coming. I dare say he won't come for a very long while, and when we can see you and Waldo we are never dull. It's only at the castle when they give us such lots of lessons and everybody is so prim and so cross if we're the least bit late. Oh, dear! —I was forgetting-shan't we be late for breakfast this morning? Is godmother coming to fetch us?'

'We are going home now,' said Waldo. 'But first we must say good-bye to the eagles. Here they are,' for as he spoke the two royal birds came circling down from overhead and settled themselves on the very edge of the cliff, whose dizzy height they calmly overlooked-their gaze fixed far beyond.

'That is where they always stay watching,' said Waldo, in a low voice, and then the children went forward till they were but a few steps behind the pair. Farther it would not have been safe to go.

'Good-bye, king and queen,' they said all together, and the eagles, slowly turning round, though without moving from their places, answered in their grave voices:

'Farewell, children. We will watch you, though you may not know it. Farewell.'

Then Waldo led the others down the rock stair by which they had come up-down past the balcony where they had had their collation of fruit, till they found themselves in the feather-lined hall.

'There is something rather sad about the eagles,' said Maia. 'Do you think it is watching so much that makes them sad?'

'Perhaps,' said Silva. 'Come and sit down here in this snug corner. Look, there is a feather arm-chair for each of us-it is a little chilly, don't you think?'

'Yes, perhaps it is. But tell me if you know why the eagles are sad.'

'I think they are more grave than sad,' replied Silva. 'I dare say watching so much does make them so.'

'Why? Do they see so far? Do they see all sorts of things?' asked Maia in a rather awe-struck tone. 'Are they like fairies, Silva?'

'I don't know exactly,' said Silva. 'But I think they are very wise, and I expect they know a great deal.'

'But they can't know as much as godmother, and she isn't sad,' said Maia.

'Sometimes she is,' said Silva. 'Besides, she has more to do than the eagles. They have only to watch-she puts things right. You'll understand better some day,' she added, seeing that Maia looked puzzled. 'But isn't it cold? Oh, see there-that's to wrap ourselves up in,' for just at this moment there flapped down on them, from no one could tell where, the great soft fluffy cloak or rug which had kept them so beautifully warm during their air-journey.

'Come under the shawl,' cried Maia to the two boys, and all the children drew their seats close together and wrapped the wonderful cloak well round them.

'But aren't we going home soon?' said Maia. 'I'm so afraid of being late.'

'Godmother knows all about it,' said Waldo. 'She's sent us this cloak on purpose. There's nothing to do but sit still-till she tells us what we're to do. I don't mind, for somehow I'm rather sleepy.'

'I think I am too,' said Rollo, and though Silva and Maia were less ready to allow it, I think they must have felt the same, for somehow or other two minutes later all the four were taking a comfortable nap, and knew nothing more till a soft clear voice whispered in their ears:

'Children, it is time to wake up.'

'Time to go home! Are the birds coming for us again?' said Maia, rubbing her eyes and staring about her. A voice softly laughing replied to her:

'Birds-what birds are you talking about? You're not awake yet, Maia, and I've been telling you to wake ever so long.'

It was Rollo.

'You, why I thought it was godmother,' said Maia; 'I heard her say, "Children, it is time to wake up," and I thought we were all in the feather-hall still. How did we get back, Rollo?'

For 'back' they were. Maia in her own little bed in the white castle, and Rollo standing beside her in his ordinary dress. Where were Waldo and Silva-where the feather-hall —where the wonderful dresses in which godmother had clothed them for the air-journey? Maia looked up at Rollo as she spoke, with disappointment in her eyes.

'We *are* back,' he said, 'and that's all there is to say about it, as far as I can see. But come, Maia, don't look so unhappy. We've had great fun, and we must be very good after it to please godmother. It's a lovely day, and after we've finished our lessons we can have some nice runs in the fields. Jump up-you're not a bit tired, are you? I'm not.'

'Nor am I,' said Maia, slowly bestirring herself. 'But I'm rather dull. I'm afraid we shan't see them again for a good while, Rollo.'

CHAPTER XII
A VISION OF CHRISTMAS TREES.

'The angels are abroad to-night.'

At Christmas-tide.

It was early summer when *we* saw them last. It is mid-winter —December-now. And winter comes in good earnest in the country where I have shown you the white castle, and told you of the doings and adventures of its two little guests. Many more could I tell you of-many a joyous summer day had they spent with their forest friends, many a wonderful dance had godmother led them, till they had got to know nearly as much as Waldo and Silva themselves of the strange happy creatures that lived in this marvellous Christmas-tree Land, and in other lands too. For as the days shortened again, and grew too cold for air-journeys and cave explorings and visits to many other denizens of the forest than I have space to tell you about, then began the season of godmother's story-tellings, which I think the children found as delightful as any other of her treats. Oh, the wonderful tales that were told round the bright little fire in Silva's dainty kitchen! Oh, the wood-fairies, and water-sprites, and dwarfs, and gnomes that they learnt about! Oh, the lovely songs that godmother sang in that witching voice of hers-that voice like none other that the children had ever heard! It was a true fairyland into which she led them —a fairyland where entered nothing ugly or cruel or mean or false, though the dwellers in it were of strange and fantastic shape and speech, children of the rainbow and the mist, unreal and yet real, like the cloud-castles that build themselves for us in the sky, or the music that weaves itself in the voice of the murmuring stream.

But even to these happy times there came an end-and the beginning of this end began to be felt when the first snow fell and Christmas-tree Land was covered with the thick white mantle it always wore till the spring's soft breath blew it off again.

'A storm is coming —a heavy storm is on its way, my darlings,' said godmother one afternoon, when she had been spinning some lovely stories for them with her invisible wheel. She had left the fireside and was standing by the open doorway, looking out at the white landscape, and as she turned round, it seemed to the children that her own face was whiter than usual-her *hair* certainly was so. It had lost the golden tinge it sometimes took, which seemed to make a gleam all over her features-so that at such times it was impossible to believe that godmother was old-and now she seemed a very tiny little old woman, as small and fragile as if she herself was made out of a snowflake, and her face looked anxious and almost sad. 'A storm is on its way,' she repeated; 'you must hasten home.'

'But why do you look so sad, godmother dear?' said Maia. 'We can get home quite safely. *You* can see to that. Nothing will ever hurt us when *you* are taking care of us.'

'But there are some things I cannot do,' said godmother, smiling, 'or rather that I would not do if I could. Times and seasons pass away and come to an end, and it is best so. Still, it may make even me sad sometimes.'

All the four pairs of eyes looked up in quick alarm. They felt that there was something-though what, they did not know-that godmother was thinking of in particular, and the first idea that came into their minds was not far from the truth.

'Godmother! oh, godmother!' exclaimed all the voices together, so that they sounded like one, 'you don't mean that we're not to see each other any more?'

'Not yet, dears, not yet,' said godmother. 'But happy times pass and sad times pass. It must be so. And, after all, why should one fret? Those who love each other meet again as surely as the bees fly to the flowers.'

'In Heaven, godmother? Do you mean in Heaven?' asked Maia, in a low voice and with a look in her eyes telling that the tears were not far off.

Godmother smiled again.

'Sooner than that sometimes. Do not look so distressed, my pretty Maia. But come now. I must get you home before the storm breaks. Kiss each other, my darlings, but it is not good-bye yet. You will soon be together again–sooner than you think.'

No one ever thought of not doing–and at once–what godmother told them. Rollo and Maia said good-bye even more lovingly than usual to their dear Waldo and Silva, and then godmother, holding a hand of each, set out on their homeward journey.

It was as she had said–the storm-spirits were in the air. Above the wind and the cracking of the branches, brittle with the frost, and the far-off cries of birds and other creatures on their way to shelter in their nests or lairs, came another sound which the children had heard of but never before caught with their own ears —a strange, indescribable sound, neither like the murmuring of the distant sea nor the growl of thunder nor the shriek of the hurricane, yet recalling all of these.

''Tis the voice of the storm,' said godmother softly. 'Pray to the good God, my darlings, for those that travel by land or sea. And now, farewell! —that beaten path between the trees will bring you out at the castle gate, and no harm will come to you. Good-bye!'

She lingered a little over the last word, and this encouraged Maia to ask a question.

'When shall we see you again, dear godmother? And will you not tell us more about why you are sad?'

'It will pass with the storm, for all is for the best,' said godmother dreamily. 'When one joy passes, another comes. Remember that. And no true joy is ever past. Keep well within shelter, my children, till the storm has had its way, and then — —' she stopped again.

'Then? What then? Oh, *do* tell us,' persisted Maia. 'You know, dear godmother, it is *very* dull in the white castle when we mayn't go out. Lady Venelda makes them give us many more lessons to keep us out of mischief, she says, and we really don't much mind. It's better to do lessons than nothing. Oh, godmother, we would have been *so* miserable here if we hadn't had you and Waldo and Silva!'

Godmother stroked Maia's sunny head and smiled down into her eyes. And something just then–was it a last ray of the setting sun hurrying off to calmer skies till the storm should have passed? —lighted up godmother's own face and hair with a wonderful glow. She looked like a beautiful young girl.

'Oh, how pretty you are!' said the children under their breath. But they were too used to these strange changes in godmother's appearance to be as astonished as many would have been.

'Three nights from now will be the day before Christmas Eve,' said godmother. 'When you go to bed look out in the snow and you will see my messenger. And remember, remember, if one joy goes, another comes. And no true joys are ever lost.'

And as they listened to her words, she was gone! So hand-in-hand, wondering what it all might mean, the children turned to the path in the snow she had shown them, which in a few minutes brought them safely home.

Though none too soon–scarcely were they within shelter when the tempest began. The wind howled, the sleet and hail dashed down, even the growling of distant thunder, or what sounded like it, was heard–the storm-spirits had it all their own way for that night and the day following; and when the second night came, and the turmoil seemed to have ceased, it had but changed its form, for the snow again began to fall, ever more and more heavily, till it lay so deep that one could hardly believe the world would ever again burst forth from its silent cold embrace.

And the white castle looked white no longer. Amid the surrounding purity it seemed gray and soiled and grimly ashamed of itself.

Three days had passed; the third night was coming.

'The snow has left off falling, and seems hardening,' Lady Venelda had said that afternoon. 'If it continues so, the children can go out to-morrow. It is not good for young people to be so long deprived of fresh air and exercise. But it is a hard winter. I only hope we shall have no more of these terrible storms before — —,' but then she stopped suddenly, for she was speaking to the old doctor, and had not noticed that Rollo and Maia were standing near.

The children had seen with satisfaction that the snow had left off falling, for, though they had faith in godmother's being able to do what no one else could, they did not quite see how she was to send them a message if the fearful weather had continued.

'We might have looked out the whole of last night without seeing anything,' said Maia, 'the snow was driving so. And if godmother means to take us anywhere, Rollo, it *is* a good thing it's so fine to-night. She was afraid of our being out in the storm the other day, you remember.'

'Because there was no need for it,' said Rollo. 'It was already time for us to be home. I'm sure she could prevent any storm hurting us if she really wanted to take us anywhere. There's Nanni coming, Maia-as soon as she's gone call me, and we'll look out together.'

Maia managed to persuade Nanni that she-Nanni, not Maia-was extra sleepy that evening, and had better go to bed without waiting to undress her. I am not quite sure that Nanni *did* go at once to bed, for the servants were already amusing themselves with Christmas games and merriment down in the great kitchen, where the fireplace itself was as large as a small room, and she naturally liked to join the fun. But all Maia cared about was to be left alone with Rollo. She called to him, and then in great excitement the two children drew back the window-curtains, and extinguishing their candles, stood hand-in-hand looking out to see what was going to happen. There was no moon visible, but it must have been shining all the same, faintly veiled perhaps behind a thin cloud, for a soft light, increased by the reflection of the spotless snow, gleamed over all. But there was nothing to be seen save the smooth white expanse, bounded at a little distance from the house by the trees which clothed the castle hill, whose forms looked strangely fantastic, half shrouded as they were by their white garment.

'There is no one-nothing there,' said Maia in a tone of disappointment. 'She must have forgotten.'

'*Forgotten* —never!' said Rollo reproachfully. 'When has godmother ever forgotten us? Wait a little, Maia; you are so impatient.'

They stood for some minutes in perfect silence. Suddenly a slight, very slight crackling was heard among the branches-so slight was it, that, had everything been less absolutely silent, it could not have been heard-and the children looked at each other in eager expectation.

'Is it Silva-or Waldo?' said Maia in a whisper. 'She said her *messenger*.'

'Hush!' said Rollo, warningly.

A dainty little figure hopped into view from the shade of some low bushes skirting the lawn. It was a robin-redbreast. He stood still in the middle of the snow-covered lawn, his head on one side, as if in deep consideration. Suddenly a soft, low, but very peculiar whistle was heard, and the little fellow seemed to start, as if it were a signal he had been listening for, and then hopped forward unhesitatingly in the children's direction.

'Did *you* whistle, Rollo?' said Maia in a whisper.

'No, certainly not. I was just going to ask if *you* did,' answered Rollo.

But now the robin attracted all their attention. He came to a stand just in front of their window, and then looked up at them with the most unmistakable air of invitation.

'We're to go with him, I'm sure we are,' said Maia, beginning to dance with excitement; 'but *how* can we get to him? All the doors downstairs will be closed, and it's far too high to jump.'

Rollo, who had been leaning out of the window the better to see the robin, suddenly drew his head in again with a puzzled expression.

'It's *very* strange,' he said. 'I'm *sure* it wasn't there this morning. Look, Maia, do you see the top of a ladder just a tiny bit at this side of the window? I could get on to it quite easily.'

'So could I,' said Maia, after peeping out. 'It's all right, Rollo. *She's* had it put there for us. Look at the robin-he knows all about it. You go first, and when you get down call to me and tell me how to manage.'

Two minutes after, Rollo's voice called up that it was all right. Maia would find it quite easy if she came rather slowly, which she did, and to her great delight soon found herself beside her brother.

'Dear me, we've forgotten our hats and jackets,' she exclaimed. 'But it's not cold-how is that?'

'*You* haven't forgotten your-what is it you've got on?' said Rollo, looking at her.

'And you-what have you got on?' said Maia in turn. 'Why, we've *both* got cloaks on, something like the shawl we had for the air-journey, only they're quite, *quite* white.'

'Like the snow-we can't be seen. They're as good as invisible cloaks,' said Rollo, laughing in glee.

'And they fit so neatly-they seem to have grown on to us,' said Maia, stroking herself. But in another moment, 'Oh, Rollo!' she exclaimed, half delighted and half frightened, 'they *are* growing, or we're growing, or something's growing. Up on your shoulders there are little *wings* coming, real little white wings-they're getting bigger and bigger every minute.'

'And they're growing on you too,' exclaimed Rollo. 'Why, in a minute or two we'll be able to fly. Indeed, I think I can fly a little already,' and Rollo began flopping about his white wings like a newly-fledged and rather awkward cygnet. But in a minute or two Maia and he found-thanks perhaps to the example of the robin, who all this time was hovering just overhead, backwards and forwards, as if to say, 'do like me' —to their great joy that they could manage quite well; never, I am sure, did two little birds ever learn to fly so quickly!

All was plain-sailing now-no difficulty in following their faithful little guide, who flew on before, now and then cocking back his dear little head to see if the two queer white birds under his charge were coming on satisfactorily. I wonder in what tribe or genus the learned men of that country, had there been any to see the two strange creatures careering through the cold wintry air, would have classed them!

But little would they have cared. Never-oh, never, if I talked about it for a hundred years-could I give you an idea of the delightfulness of being able to fly! All the children's former pleasures seemed as nothing to it. The drive in godmother's pony-carriage, the gymnastics with the squirrels, the sail in the air-all seemed nothing in comparison with it. It was so perfectly enchanting that Maia did not even feel inclined to talk about it. And on, and on, and on they flew, till the robin stopped, wheeled round, and looking at them, began slowly to fly downwards. Rollo and Maia followed him. They touched the ground almost before they knew it; it seemed as if for a moment they melted into the snow which was surrounding them here, too, on all sides, and then as if they woke up again to find themselves wingless, but still with their warm white garments, standing at the foot of an immensely high tree-for they were, it was evident, at the borders of a great forest.

The robin had disappeared. For an instant or two they remained standing still in bewilderment; perhaps, to tell the truth, a *very* little frightened, for it was much darker down here than it had been up in the air; indeed, it appeared to them that but for the gleaming snow, which seemed to have a light of its own, it would have been quite, *quite* dark.

'Rollo,' said Maia tremulously, 'hold my hand tight; don't let it go. What — —' 'Are we to do?' she would have added, but a sound breaking on the silence made her stop short.

A soft, far-away sound it was at first, though gradually growing clearer and nearer. It was that of children's voices singing a sweet and well-known Christmas carol, and somehow in the refrain at the end of each verse it seemed to Rollo and Maia that they heard their own names. 'Come, come,' were the words that sounded the most distinctly. They hesitated no longer; off they ran, diving into the dark forest fearlessly, and though it was so dark they found no difficulty. As if by magic, they avoided every trunk and stump which might have hurt them, till, half out of breath, but with a strange brightness in their hearts, they felt themselves caught round the necks and heartily kissed, while a burst of merry laughter replaced the singing, which had gradually melted away. It was Waldo and Silva of course!

'Keep your eyes shut,' they cried. 'Still a moment, and then you may open them.'

'But they're *not* shut,' objected the children.

'Ah, aren't they? Feel them,' said Waldo; and Rollo and Maia, lifting their hands to feel, found it was true. Their eyes were not only shut, but a slight, very fine gossamer thread seemed drawn across them.

'We could not open them if we would,' they said; but I don't think they minded, and they let Waldo and Silva draw them on still a little farther, till —

'Now,' they cried, and snap went the gossamer thread, and the two children stood with eyes well open, gazing on the wonderful scene around them.

They seemed to be standing in the centre of a round valley, from which the ground on every side sloped gradually upwards. And all about them, arranged in the most orderly manner, were rows and rows-tiers, perhaps, I should say-of Christmas trees-real, genuine Christmas trees of every kind and size. Some loaded with toys of the most magnificent kind, some simpler, some with but a few gifts, and those of little value. But one and all brilliantly lighted up with their many-coloured tapers-one and all with its Christmas angel at the top. And nothing in fairy-doll shape that Rollo and Maia had ever seen was so beautiful as these angels with their gleaming wings and sweet, joyous loving faces. I think, when they had a little recovered from their first astonishment, that the beauty of the tree-angels was what struck them most.

'Yes,' said a voice beside them, in answer to their unspoken thought; 'yes, each tree has *always* its angel. Not always to be seen in its true beauty-sometimes you might think it only a poor, coarsely-painted little doll. But *the* angel is there all the same. Though it is only in Santa Claus' own garden that they are to be seen to perfection.'

'Are we in Santa Claus' garden now, dear godmother?' asked Maia softly.

'Yes, dears. He is a very old friend of mine-one of my oldest friends, I may say. And he allowed me to show you this sight. No other children have ever been so favoured. By this time to-morrow night-long before then, indeed-these thousands of trees will be scattered far and wide, and round each will be a group of the happy little faces my old friend loves so well.'

'But, godmother,' said Maia practically, 'won't the tapers be burning down? Isn't it a pity to keep them lighted just for us? And, oh, dear me! however can Santa Claus get them packed and sent off in time? I *hope* he hasn't kept them too late to please us?'

Godmother smiled.

'Don't trouble your little head about that,' she said. 'But come, have you no curiosity to know which is your own Christmas-tree? Among all these innumerable ones, is there not one for you too?'

Maia and Rollo looked up in godmother's eyes-they were smiling, but something in their expression they could not quite understand. Suddenly a kind of darkness fell over everything-darkness almost complete in comparison with the intense light of the million tapers that had gleamed but an instant before-though gradually, as their eyes grew used to it, there gleamed out the same soft faint light as of veiled moonbeams, that they had remarked before.

'You can see now,' said godmother. 'Go straight on-quite straight through the trees' —for they were still in the midst of the forest —'till you come to what is waiting for you. But first kiss me, my darlings —a long kiss, for it is good-bye —and kiss, too, your little friends, Waldo and Silva, for in this world one may *hope*, but one can never be as *sure* as one would fain be, that good-byes are not for long.'

Too overawed by her tone to burst into tears, as they were yet ready to do, the children threw themselves into each other's arms.

'We *must* see each other again, we must; oh, godmother, say we shall!' cried all the four voices. And godmother, as she held them all together in her arms seemed to whisper —

'I hope it. Yes, I hope and think you will.' And then, almost without having felt that Waldo and Silva were gently but irresistibly drawn from them, Rollo and Maia found themselves again alone, hand-in-hand in the midst of the forest, as they had so often stood before. Without giving themselves time to realise that they had said good-bye to their dear little friends, off they set, as godmother had told them, running straight on through the trees, where it almost seemed by the clear though soft light that a little path opened before them as they went. Till, suddenly, for a moment the light seemed to fade and disappear, leaving them almost in darkness, which again was as unexpectedly dispersed by a wonderful brilliance, spreading and increasing, so that at first they were too dazzled to distinguish whence it came. But not for long.

'See, Rollo,' cried Maia; 'see, there is *our* Christmas tree.'

'See, Rollo,' cried Maia; 'see, there is our Christmas tree.'

And there it was-the most beautiful they had yet seen-all radiant with light and glistening with every pretty present child-heart could desire.

'We are only to *look* at it, you know,' said Maia; 'it has to be packed up and sent us, of course, like the others. But,' she stopped short, 'who is that, Rollo,' she went on, 'standing just by the tree? Can it be Santa Claus himself come to see if it is all right?'

'Santa Claus,' exclaimed a well-known voice, 'Santa Claus, indeed! Is that your new name for me, my Maia?'

Then came a cry of joy —a cry from two little loving hearts —a cry which rang merry echoes through the forest, and at which, though it woke up lots of little birds snugly hidden away in the warmest corners they could find, no one thought of grumbling, except, I think, an old owl, who greatly objected to any disturbance of his nightly promenades and meditations.

'Papa, papa, dear papa!' was the cry. 'Papa, you have come back to us. *That* was what god-mother meant,' they said together. And their father, well pleased, held them in his arms as if he would never again let them go.

'So you have learnt to know what godmother means-that is well,' he said. 'But kiss me once more only, just now, my darlings, and then you must go home and sleep till the morning. And keep it a secret that you have seen me to-night.'

He kissed them again, and before their soft childish lips had left his face, a strange dreamy feeling overpowered them. Neither Rollo nor Maia knew or thought anything more of where they were or how they had come there for many hours.

And then they were awakened-Rollo first, then Maia-by the sound of Nanni's delighted voice at their bedside.

'Wake up, wake up,' she said, 'for the most beautiful surprise has come to you for this happy Christmas Eve.'

And even without her telling them, they knew what it was-they knew who was waiting for them downstairs, nor could all their awe of Lady Venelda prevent them rushing at their father and hugging him till he was nearly choked. But Lady Venelda, I must confess, was too happy herself to see her kinsman again to be at all vexed with them. And her pleasure, as well as that of the kind old doctor, was increased by the thanks they received for all their care of the children, whom their father declared he had never seen so bright or blooming.

And, a few days afterwards, they went back with him to their own happy home; and what then? —did they ever see godmother and Waldo and Silva again? I can only answer, like god-mother herself, 'I hope so; yes, I hope so, and think so.' But as to how or where-ah, that I cannot say!

THE END.

Made in United States
North Haven, CT
10 December 2021